The Suicidal Peanut

The Suicidal Peanut

Matthew J. Metzger

queerteen
QT

THE SUICIDAL PEANUT

JMS Books LLC
10286 Staples Mill Rd. #221
Glen Allen, VA 23060
www.jms-books.com

Printed in the United States of America

ISBN: 9781515308256

Chapter 1

PORTRAITURE.

Tab stared at the assignment title, and mentally swore off praying to the God of Comic Art. He obviously wasn't pulling his weight. Tab had been praying diligently for *months* for the thirty-percent assignment (with five percent exhibition, because the God of Public Appearances hated him and wanted to make sure he suffered) to be comic art. Or even any stylised form at all. There was so much flexibility in those modules, but...

But *portraiture?* Tab hated portraits. They had to look halfway realistic, and Tab didn't *do* realism. Halfway or otherwise.

"That," Maxi said, plonking their cardboard coffee cups on the table, and barely missing covering the stupid assignment sheet in lukewarm mocha, "is so much better than I'd expected."

Tab rolled his eyes. Of *course* Maxi would say that. Maxi was all about the drawing of the people. Any people. Preferably people who weren't really aware of it at the time, because Maxi was kind of a stalker if you thought about it. Of hot boys, mostly, but occasionally girls with hairstyles she wanted to copy, or The Dancing Redhead, a girl from the dance department of the college that Maxi had her one and only lesbian crush on.

Tab fished the assignment sheet out from the mess Maxi always made of any table she sat at, and stashed it away.

"Who are you going to draw?" he asked.

"Alice," Maxi said promptly. "Obviously. I'm going to bring some disability awareness to this exhibition. Are you aware in the last *eight* exhibitions, there's not been a single disabled person?"

"…And?"

"Tab! There's only *been* eight!"

"Well, maybe nobody else knows any disabled people."

Maxi snorted.

"Or maybe the disabled people don't *want* to be drawn."

"Alice will, she loves the attention," Maxi beamed. Alice was her fourteen-year-old sister, whose expression of any emotion whatsoever was a garbled sort of grunting. Maxi swore she could talk; Tab wasn't convinced. But then, he'd only met (seen) Alice twice. She didn't like strangers, apparently, and Tab was totally fine with that. "So?"

"Huh?"

"Stop going off in your own little world," Maxi scoffed. "Who are you going to draw, eh?"

Tab shrugged. "I dunno."

"You must know."

"I don't. I hate doing portraits. Or real people. They get offended and shit."

"So draw someone who doesn't know," Maxi winked, and tracked her eyes around the café. She had sharp, purposeful eyes; they always *watched*, and never simply *were*. The reason? *Slaaag.* Maxi was a flirt. End of, really. Maxi was the high priestess at the Temple of the Flirt, and Tab had every intention of drawing her one day as an acolyte of Lust or something when he was a famous comic book artist. (Or a cartoonist, he hadn't quite decided yet.)

Maxi was the kind of girl who was easy to draw in a comic style. She was all curves and long curly hair (technically dark brown, but she religiously dyed it black) and oversized hipster glasses even though she didn't actually need glasses. She wore off-the-shoulder tops a lot, too, because (she said) it showed off her nice shoulders and long neck and (everyone else said) it showed the cleavage that you could smother a man in. She'd make an *awesome* villainess. Tab just had no intention of ever telling her that. The ego was big enough already.

"Tab!"

He jumped; Maxi huffed and adjusted her huge glasses. "We seriously need to find you a boyfriend," she despaired. "Don't you have a crush on anyone? Like *anyone*? Even seen someone wearing really nice jeans that were ironed at some point in their lives?"

"No," Tab lied.

She huffed. "Do you even *know* any other gay guys around here?"

"Uncle Eddie," he said, quick as a flash.

"Gay guys that *aren't* members of your own family, Tab," Maxi said, and flicked his forehead. "Nerd. Come on, don't you? You must. You do, right?"

"Not anyone I'd ever date," he said more truthfully. He'd gone to, like, one LGBT meeting at the college. It had been full of potato-shaped lesbians with brutal haircuts and weirdly deep voices, and lanky gay guys who talked with a lisp and carried fashion magazines under one arm. (And okay, it was an arts college, but still…) Nobody Tab had really felt comfortable talking to—it had been *excruciating*, actually—and then they'd all voted to go get trollied, and Tab felt awkward enough in public without being drunk.

"Well," Maxi prodded him in the arm, hunching forward like they were sharing secrets. They kind of were. Tab never talked about his crushes with anyone, really. It was just kind of awkward with Uncle Eddie, and he never knew what to say to Aunt JuliKate anyway, and everyone who knew he was gay had guessed. He'd never even technically come out of the closet. Maybe there *was* no closet. He was just kind of…auto-out. "What's your type?"

Dangerous, gorgeous, and preferably half-naked. "I dunno."

"Oh come *on*, Tab! Look," Maxi leaned across, her curly hair flopping forward over the table in a waterfall. A bubbly one. With dandruff. Tab moved his coffee. "I could set you up, you know."

"Oh no. No, no, no, no."

"Taaaaab."

"Maxi, I'm not going on a blind date."

"What if I *promise* it's with a nice guy and…"

"No!" Tab insisted.

She huffed, and folded her arms under her chest. Half the room paid attention to the manoeuvre. "So how are you going to find some cute guy to draw for the portraiture assignment and start dating a literal model, then?" she demanded.

"I *won't*," Tab said shortly.

Because there was no way the model he had in mind was *ever* going to date him.

WELCOME TO GRANGEFIELDS Boxing and Martial Arts Gym.

This gym operates a strict no-harassment policy. Any student found using or displaying sexist, homophobic, racist, transphobic or ableist language or attitudes will be excluded with immediate effect.

All visitors must sign in at reception upon arrival.

If this door is locked between 8 A.M. and 7 P.M., ring bell at bottom of stairs.

Not that the bell worked. Or the door was locked between those hours. Or ever, really.

Grangefields was the enormous roof space of a converted warehouse, a mechanics' garage underneath, and the roof space split into two-thirds for the gym, and the remaining third for the flat. The entire top floor was owned by Tab's Uncle Eddie, but though Eddie ran the gym, Aunt JuliKate ran the flat. With an iron fist, decorated in ugly rings.

Tab had come to live with Uncle Eddie (and by default Aunt JuliKate) when he'd been accepted at the arts college. He'd escaped Loonyville, Mumshire (seriously, Mum had changed her name to Serenity Moonchild and used to go out on the full moon to dance naked around rocks and shit) to move in with Uncle Eddie, and not being woken at one in the morning to have his dreams analysed or join in an impromptu séance was a small price to pay for working in the gym. That had been Uncle Eddie's offer. Man the reception desk, help out with the cleaning in the evening, and have a rent-free room in the flat.

And, really, what other choice had Tab had? He'd been only just sixteen, and Mum was…gone, really. The other option had been Nana, or some kind of scabby youth hostel for kids coming out of care, and *fuck* that, pardon his Klingon. So Uncle Eddie and the job it had been.

Tab didn't really mind. The boxing students didn't hang about and bother him, so he got to sit behind the desk and draw.

The door at the top of the stairs opened into a little lobby with a reception desk, walls covered in posters and framed awards, and a couple of sofas clustered in a corner, usually used by those who drove to the gym and needed to recover after one of Marcus' bag-work classes. Off the lobby sprouted the changing rooms, the weights room, the training room, and the bag room. Tab was yet to work out why a boxing gym needed so many rooms, but then he'd rather visit the dentist for a root canal than box. Tab didn't do contact sports. Or any sports more tiring than darts, really. Or darts. Darts involved pointy things…

It was Wednesday; the intermediate class was due to start in half an hour, so Tab went straight into the lobby rather than return to the flat. It was empty. Uncle Eddie was still finishing off with the beginners, and none of the intermediates had arrived—and Tab wasn't going to risk missing them.

He was in the intermediate class.

If Tab liked going to art college and living with his (slightly) more sane aunt and uncle, then—actually—he *loved* his job. Not for the job itself. The job was boring, in all honesty. Uncle Eddie hated doing 'that mundane crap' and when Aunt JuliKate had started hor-mone replacement therapy, it had made her pretty sick for ages, so Tab had been given her old duties, pretty much. Which involved, ninety percent of the time, sitting behind a desk staring at the wall.

But he loved it. Because, not ten minutes after Tab arrived, *he* walked in.

Tab was tuned to this: the clink of the door as a boy with a black sports bag, dark blue jeans, and a zipped-up hooded sweatshirt am-bled into the gym, pausing long enough to etch his signature onto the attendance sheet on the front desk, and then banging through to the changing rooms and totally ignoring Tab in the process.

Him.

He had no name. Tab didn't know his name, and giving him one seemed sacrilege. His name, whatever it was, would be *perfect*, and maybe just a little bit exotic, because he looked vaguely Italian (stocky and dark hair and eyebrows, though he shaved his head and he wasn't greasy). But anyway. It wasn't like they were ever going to talk. He might be the most gorgeous guy Tab had ever seen, and Tab most definitely had a crush a thousand miles wide on him, but…

But, well. Look at him. He was obviously, totally, one hundred percent, holy-shit-heterosexual, and given that he was like eighteen and an intermediate-level boxer and came to the extra fitness and bagwork classes on Thursday evenings, Tab was pretty sure that the mystery stunner could also kill people with his face. Especially gay people who had crushes on him.

It was one of those…boy-meets-boy-who-is-totally-going-to-kill-him-if-he-finds-out kind of things. Only without the happy ending, because, sadly, there wasn't a God of Turning People Gay.

So Tab never asked. He kept it quiet, and didn't breathe a single word of his crush, no matter how tempting it was. No matter how much he dreamed, and prayed to his gods, and *hoped*. A futile hope, but he did it anyway.

It never stopped Tab looking though. Or dreaming. Because he was stunning. Tab had seen him in boxing shorts and gloves and nothing else, and that was the stuff dreams (all varieties) were made of. A six-pack, but so lightly defined and wiry that he didn't look bulked out until he *lashed* out. Shaved-down hair and slightly wild dark eyebrows that were always raised with the fists, giving him this totally 'come at me, bro' face, and a legit one, because Tab had watched him fight, too, and it was brutal. A long nose, but not sticking out; it had been broken in the middle, but not bent; a mouth crooked in a gorgeous kind of way, wide and messy, like he'd have a killer smile if he wanted to, and an oval face that was both steely and yielding. No square jaw or buttcrack-chin on him, no way. He was perfect.

(Tab had been icily informed by JuliKate that the boy in question was, in fact, just another kid getting his face smashed in by treated leather, but what the hell did JuliKate know?)

Okay, so he wasn't very tall (maybe five eight, way shorter than Uncle Eddie) but he was fast and lethal and had probably won professional matches and everything, Tab was sure of it. And he had cheekbones that could cut glass, and probably people's faces. Between the cheekbones and the eyebrows, the 'come at me, bro' face was common, and sometimes accompanied by the 'oh really?' face and the 'I can't believe what I'm hearing' face, and all three were horribly kissable. And the week Tab had arrived, he'd gotten concussed and Tab had had to hold an ice pack on his head until a paramedic arrived, and he had these beautiful green eyes that were flecked with little specks of gold and brown and...

So maybe Aunt JuliKate had a point when she said Tab 'mooned' over 'that short lad in the middle group.' But so what? It wasn't like Tab was ever going to get anywhere with his mooning. The gayest things about the object of said mooning were those cheekbones. And maybe those amazing dark eyelashes around those eyes. And that was it. He probably beat up gay people for shits and giggles in his down time. He was not, never could be, and never would be gay.

End. Of. Story.

So Tab had never so much as said hi. The odd time he had nodded at Tab, Tab's heart had exploded and he'd tried to hide under the desk. They'd never talked, and they were never going to, because between the fact that the God of Public Appearances hated Tab, and the God of Looking Cool In Front Of Your Crushes (and let's lump the Luck God in there as well, because *he* was an arse too, as Tab never *had* any luck) thought it was funny to toy with him...

In short, Tab was never, ever, *ever* going to get beyond even the vaguest fantasies about The Gorgeous Maybe-Italian Boxer.

But he *was* going to draw the boxer for the portraiture assignment. Even if—and it would—it spelled certain death.

Chapter 2

MAXIBABY: SOOOOO, FOUND your model yet? ;)

"Andy, don't use your tablet at the table," Aunt JuliKate said, and plonked a bowl of spaghetti in front of him.

ADEQUATEHEROES: Gimme more than half a day, Jesus!

"S'not Andy, Kate," he grumbled, propping the tablet against his glass of Coke and sticking a fork into the coils of what he'd called worms until he was about ten. "Thanks."

"Mm," she hummed. "Eddie! Get your arse in 'ere, God's sake!"

Tab grimaced at the hoarse shout. Aunt JuliKate would be Aunt Kate in a few months, though she'd started out life in the Barnes family as Uncle Julian. And when she bellowed at Uncle Eddie, the voice coaching totally failed and she dropped, like, an octave. And a half.

She also called him Andy. Like Andy Murray. Because Tab's first name was *awful* (thanks a lot, Mum) and sounded like 'tennis' and then-Uncle Julian had just about laughed himself sick when Eddie had told him the story of Tab becoming 'Tab' and not some dead probably gay bloke *(thanks,* Uncle Eddie) and Julian had dubbed him Andy Murray on the spot.

God only knew why, to be honest. Tab didn't look like Andy Murray. (Thank God.) Tab actually styled his hair for one, and he wore glasses (but proper ones, not like Maxi's silly ones) and he didn't like stupid sports with obscure rules. Okay, so Tab had brown hair, but that was hardly a reason to liken him to Andy Murray.

But you couldn't tell Aunt JuliKate *anything*, so yeah. Andy. He'd been 'Andy' ever since that day. He hated it, because his first crush ever had been called Andy, and Tab had hated him for having a girlfriend and being generally so bloody *nice* about the whole fiasco and, most of all, being *straight*. Heterosexual bastard.

> MAXIBABY: Pur-leeeeez, Tab! You totes had someone in mind! ;) Tell me!!

> ADEQUATEHEROES: I might see if one of the guys at the gym would let me take a photo and use that. Portrait in motion, you know? Thinking I might break out the charcoal.

"Andy!"

"Sorry," he mumbled around a mouthful of worms, and ducked Uncle Eddie's enormous paw as he stumbled into the kitchen and attempted to ruffle Tab's hair, still steaming from the shower. JuliKate rolled her eyes, but accepted the offered kiss on the cheek with grudging grace.

Eddie and JuliKate were like chalk and cheese, even before Julian started becoming Kate. Eddie was a six foot bear of a man with about ten percent of his skin still visible under a billion tattoos, and built like a brick shithouse. He went running every morning, taught an extremely physical sport, and ate only granola bars, chocolate, and kiwi smoothies during the working day. JuliKate, on the other hand, was a leggy, lithe silhouette with delicate features, elegant hands, and hips made for a luau. Neither Julian nor Kate would ever have *dreamed* of tattooing that flawless skin. Of course, the final nail in the twink coffin was that JuliKate worked at a hair salon, which was just so *stereotypical*.

But it did mean Tab got free, in-style haircuts every month. So that was cool.

"How was your day, kid?"

MAXIBABY: A fit gay boxer?

"Okay," Tab mumbled, tapping out a reply. *No such thing.*

MAXIBABY: All boxers are fit!

ADEQUATEHEROES: The gay bit, dipshit.

MAXIBABY: Still saying I could set you up ;)

"Andy, for goodness' sake."

"Leave him alone, Kate," Eddie said—or, well, probably said, through the hamster impression he was doing. Seriously. It went against the laws of physics to get that much spaghetti in your mouth, right? Maybe Tab should draw Uncle Eddie eating and gross out the examiners.

…Nah. He'd lose points if they threw up in the middle of his exhibition. Plus *he* might throw up.

ADEQUATEHEROES: And how many gay guys do you know???

Genuine question, really. He'd met Maxi on their first day in art college, and though they'd hit it off—or rather, she'd adopted him and he'd gone along with it in startled silence for about a month—he really didn't know *that* much about her. She had that super villainess talent of running at the mouth without actually *saying* anything, or saying totally useless stuff. Tab knew her bra size and her favourite eyeshadow, but didn't so much as know her birthday.

MAXIBABY: Pft, my brother's gay, superhero! I'm sure he has a nice ex somewhere ;)

Tab rolled his eyes.

ADEQUATEHEROES: Woo, Jones cast-offs. I can hardly wait.

MAXIBABY: :P Or a jones! You'd like Demi, he's a dork just like you!

Tab grimaced. Maxi teased him enough about being a dork without setting him up with this Demi guy. He'd never met Maxi's brother. He knew she had one—she was a twin, and seemed to think it made her psychic when it came to her brother, for whatever reason—but Tab had never met him. Or even seen a picture of him. Tab just imagined some frizzy-haired, lanky guy with hipster glasses. And massive boobs.

Not. Attractive.

"Andy, eat your tea and stop gossiping," JuliKate swatted him with a napkin; he ignored her, hefting a forkful of spaghetti into his mouth and tapping away.

> ADEQUATEHEROES: Date him or draw him? Either way, draw/date a male you—not my hottest fantasy.
>
> MAXIBABY: Arsehole. You'd lurrrrrrrrv me if you were straight.
>
> ADEQUATEHEROES: MASSIVE if.
>
> MAXIBABY: :((((

Tab rolled his eyes. He could almost *hear* the dramatics. Who was he kidding? Famous comic strip artist would be easy, he just had to follow Maxi everywhere drawing her histrionics. "Weirdo," he mumbled to himself.

Eddie eyed him over a forkful of spaghetti and said, "S'up?"

"Maxi's trying to set me up."

"...Who?"

"Maxi," Tab repeated, and sighed. "At college?"

"Frizzy hair? Tits?" Eddie asked, and then, "Hey!" as JuliKate tried to hit him with her napkin, which probably cunningly concealed her spoon in it, too.

"Yes," Tab said.

"Long as the brother don't have tits, what's the problem?"

"I've never met him."

"Gotta meet 'em at some point, kid," Eddie said serenely. "Figured you'd pick someone up at college, but hey, you gotta get going. Get started. Gotta be practical."

"Practical?" Tab dared.

"No such thing as love at first sight," Eddie retorted. "Your Mum's a fruitcake and don't forget it—there isn't no fairytale ending or first love or none of that shit. You get lust at first sight, sure, and if you're *lucky* you'll find someone who can actually put the fuck up with you, but love comes a whole lot later. So get practising. Get flirting, get fucking, and one day you'll realise you don't want to sneak out before he wakes up beside you."

"Oh my God," JuliKate moaned, and slapped her head into the palm of her hand. Tab huffed, rolling his eyes to the ceiling (like any of his wayward gods were even *listening* because *hello*, that was prime intervention moment *right fucking there,* Jesus!) and went back to his tablet.

"I'm not even going to *answer* that," he said, and told Maxi, *Pics or your brother is made up.*

> MAXIBABY: He is NOT.

> ADEQUATEHEROES: So pics.

> MAXIBABY: Fine, Jesus. Hang on.

"You are such a harsh, sceptical, narrow-minded…" JuliKate was saying, and Eddie was calmly munching his way through piles of overdone spaghetti.

"But it's *true,*" he insisted.

Tab knew it wasn't true. Love existed. And it *could* happen just like that—it had happened to Uncle Eddie just like that, whatever he said. One minute he'd been married to Auntie Anna, and the next there'd been a divorce and 'Tab, this is Julian' and Mum had said something about soulmates. (Tab didn't remember much, he'd not been very old at the time.) But anyway. Love *did* just happen sometimes. And he was pretty sure if he actually mustered up the courage to talk to the guy in the gym, just once, he'd be in love proper.

Only it was never going to happen, so…

The tablet pinged, and a picture popped up from Maxi. A not particularly well-taken picture from a holiday on a random beach somewhere, Alice's wheelchair on promenade boards, Maxi and her brother standing either side of it and grinning, their other sister (Tab couldn't remember her name, but Alice's twin) cross-legged in front of the chair and beaming obnoxiously, like a mini-Maxi. Frizzy hair and all. They *all* had frizzy hair.

Demi Jones, then, was not particularly interesting. Like Maxi, he was fair-skinned, curly-haired, and of rather average height and build, although it was a bit hard to tell in loose swimming trunks to his knees (complete with Hawaiian flowers) and a baggy T-shirt. Sunglasses obscured most of his face, and he had a wide smile showing off a set of irritatingly perfect teeth. The picture was obviously a bit dated (Maxi's hair was only at her shoulders, not her frigging *waist*) but it was enough, really, to be able to say that Demi was...

ADEQUATEHEROES: Meh, he's alright.

MAXIBABY: Awwww, he's pouting at you! :(DON'T MAKE MY BROTHER POUT!

Tab squinted at the picture again and grinned. *Is that a Star Wars T-shirt?*

MAXIBABY: He says yes. Dorkage. DORKAGE.

ADEQUATEHEROES: So he's into crappy science fiction?

MAXIBABY: I quote: 'It's all crappy, that's what makes it good.' I have no idea. Is that a dork thing???

Tab sniggered as JuliKate removed his plate and sighed at his tendency to weed out the tomatoes. *Yes,* he said, wandering back into the main room and flopping across the sofa. Uncle Eddie had an evening class at six, and JuliKate liked to gossip on the phone in the master bedroom most evenings. Mostly bitching about her psychiatrist, as far as Tab could tell.

MAXIBABY: See you're both losers, you should hook up!

ADEQUATEHEROES: Thanks but no thanks, Maxi.

Quite aside from Demi Jones being adequate-looking at best,

and losing some serious points for sharing genes with Maxi (because Tab loved Maxi, he really did, but *oh my God* she was such an overbearing, bossy cow at times) Tab was a romantic. He wanted eyes to meet across a crowded room, and pulses racing before they even said hello, and really, really hot sex. Like in the movies.

Okay, so he was a shallow romantic. Still counts.

> ADEQUATEHEROES: Stop trying to run my love life before sorting out your own!

> MAXIBABY: PRICK!

Tab sat back, changed the channel on the telly, and watched her rant. It would get rid of her, and her dorky brother, and all her intentions for...at *least* ten minutes.

THE DOUBLE-WHAMMY of the portraiture assignment was, well, Tab hadn't actually *done* any portraiture since his first six weeks at college. Art at secondary school had consisted of drawing pans in varying lights. Usually badly. And every now and then taking a picture on his mobile and pretending it was artistically bad instead of just shit. (Somehow, he'd actually pulled that one off, but he'd never worked out how.)

He spent most of the next morning, therefore, sitting with his feet up on the reception desk and sketching loosely on his pad. It was his moving-out gift from Mum, even though he hadn't so much moved out as...well, never mind. It was a gift from Mum anyway. She'd been nuts, but at least she had always kept him supplied with big, high-quality sketchpads and a range of inks, before...well, before the relapse and the hospital and...

Anyway. By the time Uncle Eddie ambled out of the training room with the cleaning supplies and headed back into the flat to catch a quick breakfast before the first class, Tab had inked the careful outline of a single eye in enormous, delicate detail.

"That's pretty good, kid," Eddie said on his way past. "When the intermediates get here, ship 'em into the bag room. Floor's still damp in the others."

"Mm," Tab hummed, exchanging the thick nib for a thinner specimen and beginning the long, light flicks of eyelashes curving up in a rich arc from the upper lid. The Sydney Harbour bridge, perhaps.

"Worse'n your mother," Eddie grumbled, and headed out.

Tab ignored him. He got his artistic streak from Mum, sure, but he liked to think his father had been sane. Or maybe that came from Uncle Eddie, given that his dad was apparently equally nutty and into dancing around rocks naked as Mum. (Tab was pretty sure he was conceived on a rock, under the full moon, probably somewhere in the middle of freakin' Ireland.)

Tab had been drawing comics—shitty ones, at least—since he could hold a pen. He'd been drawing comics of Mum saving the world from capitalism and energy companies and the police since before he could write his own name. (Well, to be fair, it was a hell of a name to ask of a four-year-old.) He hadn't known what capitalism or energy companies looked like, and all the comics had Mum in a weird purple cape the same colour as her favourite dream-catcher, and 'the police' was always PC Thorpe who'd worked their area and used to give Tab chocolate on the sly and was actually dead nice, but…meh. The thought counted. And PC Thorpe was about six foot six so he'd been easy to make into an evil policeman for Tab's crappy comics.

As he switched the black ink for the yellow and began to carefully draw tiny circles of gold into the very edges of the iris, Tab considered that if only the assignment didn't have such horribly strict criteria, he could get away with a huge eye and call it portraiture. After all, it was…

"Oi."

The God of Not Looking Like A Prat In Front Of Your Crush was frowning on him, because…well. Tab hadn't heard anyone come in, so engrossed was he in getting the gold flecks in just the right places, that he shrieked, flung the pad into the air, and dived off the chair and onto the lino with a hard and painful smack.

"Ow," said the voice. "You alright?"

Tab rubbed his elbow, grimaced, and looked up. Right into the gorgeous, amazing, god-like, *perfect* face of…of *him*. With those stunning, hazel-and-green eyes that had perfectly round gold flecks in them.

And as if in slow motion, the pad came down, wide open and sailing gaily through the air on a self-made breeze, and a gloved hand shot out to catch it.

"Bloody hell," he said, turning the eye the right way up. He whistled. "Not bad, mate."

Tab gaped like a landed goldfish.

"Er," the boy said, raising an eyebrow at him. Lust and embarrassment declared war and hoisted their flags on each side of the battlefield. "You alright?"

"Yes," Tab blurted out. "I…fucking hell, yeah, I'm fine, you just…you just…I didn't hear you come in! I didn't hear you!"

He shrugged. "Sorry, mate. Door was open. Here."

And he extended a hand down over the desk. Lust and embarrassment retired from the field. There wasn't room, after all, for a battle while Tab was having *a fucking heart attack*.

"Jesus, you hit your head?" the cause of said heart attack rasped, and leaned down far enough to seize Tab's T-shirt at the shoulder and haul. When the cotton made a threatening noise, Tab's survival instincts (JuliKate *hated* torn clothes) kicked in and he scrambled up, the boxer's hand transferring seamlessly to his arm to pull him the rest of the way.

Holy shit. Holybloodyfuckingterminalshit. *He* was touching Tab. Through leather gloves, but it counted. *He* had touched his sketch. *He* had *seen* the sketch, seen Tab's drawing *of his own eye*. *He'd* talked to him. *He* had a deep raspy voice, like sand over rocks. In a sandstorm. Tab had never liked the desert before.

"Alright?"

"Um, yes, thanks, I'm fine, Jesus," Tab scrubbed both hands over his face and sat down in the chair again heavily.

"You're Eddie's nephew, aintcha?"

"Um, yes. Yes," Tab offered, scrambling for the sign-in list. Well. A bit of paper anyway. He should have set it out. He should have set it out before he started drawing.

"Seriously? You're kinda…not so fucking intimidating."

"Yes," Tab said tartly. "Um, and you? I don't…we've never…you know, you never said hi before."

The oh-my-God-he's-talking-to-me-what-the-hell guy shrugged. "Never needed to. Cheers," he added, when Tab finally found the sign-in sheet and pushed it forward. "Um, pen?"

Tab handed over the yellow fineliner. The boy eyed it for a second before shrugging and scrawling an unreadable signature. "So?" Tab prompted.

"Oh," he said, capping the pen and handing it back, along with the sketchpad *He* still held in one gloved fist. "Nick," he said, and grinned. Two stubs of broken front teeth beamed out at Tab, a twisted canine beside them, and yet they were dangerously beautiful because it was *his*—no, *Nick's* smile.

Tab smoothed out the sketch as Nick disappeared into the changing rooms, and reached for the green pen.

Screw what Uncle Eddie said. He was totally, *totally* in love.

With a gorgeous, faux-Italian guy called Nick.

Chapter 3

"BECAUSE," TAB FUMBLED, staring at the loops and whorls of the statuette, "it's not just one being, is it? It's, um, it's two beings. Only they're joined as one because, um…um, the idea is that people together are more powerful than people apart. That *love* is more powerful than…um, I don't know, than like magnetism for joining stuff up. For good."

The God of Totally Winging It eyed the sculpture sceptically…then nodded. One of Tab's few benefactors. "Very good," the lecturer smiled. "Does anyone have a rebuttal for that approach?"

Tab couldn't care less, and dropped his gaze back to his pad. He'd offer up a sacrifice to the God of Totally Winging It when he got home. For now, he had ideas to get on the paper.

He'd been sketching round things all through her wittering on (he couldn't care *less* about postmodernist sculpture!) practising for the gloves on his portrait. For when he could eventually get some actual luck and get a picture of Nick boxing. And not get his face boxed, or the attention of the God of Being Beaten Up By Crushes on a bad day. (He *had* been beaten up by a crush once, and it had bloody hurt. But it *had* made the crush go away, so…)

"Weasel," Maxi whispered, and peered at his paper. "Got ideas, then?"

"Mm."

"Who're you drawing?"

"None of yours."

"Might be."

"Miss Jones, am I interrupting?"

"Sorry," Maxi said. Liar. "Just so you know," she added in a lower whisper. "My offer stands. I could totally hook you up with Demi."

"With your loser brother? No thanks."

"He's cuuuuute," Maxi said encouragingly.

So was Nick. *Beyond* cute. And Tab could dream, right? Who needed boyfriends when you had dream boyfriends? Dream boyfriends didn't forget anniversaries or birthdays, and they always brought presents and flowers, and paid for the date, and didn't get jealous or grumpy or bored, and…okay, maybe they didn't actually talk to you, you know, in real *life*, but who needed real life? Tab's fantasy life was doing so much *better* than that. Tab's fantasy life was *awesome*.

"Male you, and he was meh."

"His boyfriend doesn't think he's meh," Maxi said in a snotty tone. "I'll give you his number."

She tried to take his phone; Tab snatched it back. "No. And why would I want to be set up with a guy who *has a boyfriend?*"

"Because his boyfriend is a complete dick," Maxi said seriously, and huffed. The college bell rang, and she gathered her papers into her ample chest. They crumpled feebly. "Seriously, he's such a jerk, and Demi just *lets* him be a jerk, I've *told* him to dump him on his gay arse, but…"

Tab tuned her out, staunchly protecting his phone by putting it into the zipped pocket of his bag as they headed towards their favourite café. It was sunny, but really cold, and he huddled into his jacket and wondered if it would be okay if he bailed on Maxi and went to the gym early. He could turn the little space heater on under the desk and warm his feet, and draw comics for a bit. The Inspiration Acolytes had been buzzing since that morning, and he flipped open his sketchbook again as they found a table.

"Cappuccino?"

"Please. Extra shot of espresso?"

"Got it."

It was January. The assignment was due only three days before Tab's eighteenth, and Maxi was already making noises about doing something. Tab didn't want to—he was awkward with people, and he didn't relish the idea of a big party like the ones Maxi threw—but then maybe he should let her organise something little. Pub drinks or something. Maybe…Tab toyed with the edges of his page of doodles. Maybe he should let her plan something, and drag her gay brother to it. Maybe he wouldn't have a boyfriend anymore, and that Tab had reached almost-eighteen without ever having a boyfriend was *criminal*. It was *abnormal* and *wrong* and *weird* and it wasn't like Nick was going to spontaneously go gay just in time for Tab's birthday. Or, you know, ever.

"There," Maxi plonked the cups down. "But like I was saying, Demi seriously needs to dump his boyfriend. The guy *cheated* on him last summer, and Demi just let him get away with it!"

"What a jerk," Tab said obediently. He was half-listening. He wasn't blessed much, but the Demons of Procrastination were his friends, and one of them was named…well, whatever the ancient Aramaic word for 'listening with half an ear' was.

"Even Mum doesn't like him," Maxi continued, stirring her coffee noisily. "I mean, Mum likes everybody, she even likes you and she's never met you, so…"

"Uh-huh."

"I mean, he claims he really likes this one—and I *want* to say give love a chance and everything, right…"

"Sounds nice."

"But he *cheated*, Tab, that's just shit!"

"What a cunt."

"You're not even listening."

"Huh?"

"Exactly," Maxi said loftily, sipping at her coffee. "You never are once you get scribbling. *What* are you scribbling?"

"Mm," Tab hummed, fishing for a different, thicker pencil and finding a stub. It would do; he started to sketch the road and traffic lights outside. It was the main road running into town, but the lights changed every thirty seconds because of all the college students wandering off into the housing estate on the other side.

"So did you ask your boxer if you could take a picture?"

"Haven't seen him since," Tab lied.

"Taaaaab," Maxi whined, and prodded him in the arm with a fingernail like a claw. "You need to get that sorted, you know. You do *so* many build-up sketches; it takes you *ages* to…"

"I know," he mumbled, drawing a thick circle for the green light. He didn't like it, and used tiny, flicking lines for the amber one. "I can start practising portraiture without him, though."

"So, what's his name?"

"No, Maxi."

"No? That's a weird name."

He rolled his eyes at her; she simply beamed back and eyed his traffic lights. "You're not finding out," he said.

"Why not?" she pouted.

"Because you'll cause trouble and try to come to the gym and tell him."

"Of course I will!" she said, and Tab sighed. Really, did she have to be so *honest?* She really would make an amazing villainess. Maybe he could write her into his first big comic series, once he was a really famous artist. Or into his cartoon strip, when he was a famous cartoonist. Maybe launch a whole new strip with her. He could imagine the revealing costume now. And her name would have to be a pun on Maxi. Or tampon. "You totally fancy him."

"Which is totally irrelevant, because he's *straight,"* Tab insisted.

"Why can't you find a guy here? There's loads of gay guys here. Half the dance group are gay."

"Yeah, the male half," Tab smirked, and turned the tables. "Not your sexy redhead."

"Oh shut your face," she blew on her coffee, but pinked delicately. "You seriously need a boyfriend."

"And you don't?"

"I'm a strong, independent woman and I do not need a man to

complete me," she recited faithfully. *"You* are a sad lonely dweeb who draws comics all day and has a crush on a straight guy."

"Who could break my face."

"Who could break your face," she agreed.

"Doesn't mean I'm going to date your brother."

"Or even just *talk* to him?"

"Or even that," Tab insisted ruthlessly. "I'm not hitting on a guy I've never met, who looks about average, and who has a boy-friend. Which, ironically, would make him a cheater, too, and not just his dick of a boyfriend. See? I *was* listening."

Maxi pouted, but Tab was resolute. There was no *point.* And anyway, even if Maxi's brother was drop-dead gorgeous, he wasn't *Nick.*

"It's not happening," he said, and started shading the red traffic light with dots. He liked that method. Maybe he'd draw Nick in dots.

"You suck," Maxi informed him.

Outside, the skies belched, and it began to rain.

TAB GOT BACK to the gym in the middle of the advanced class. Through the glass doors, he could see them all crowding round a demonstration, and waved to Uncle Eddie before taking up position behind the desk. Aunt JuliKate usually covered it when he was at college, but she was nowhere to be seen.

He settled back, abandoning his doodles on the counter, and logged on to the gym wi-fi system. He had an email from the charity who'd stepped in when Mum had started to…well, step out, and he saved it into the *Mum Stuff* folder for reading later—much later, because Mum stuff was depressing stuff—and a couple of junk mails about art degrees in America. No way was he going to America. There had never been a hot American guy in the history of ever (no matter what Maxi said about half-a-dozen actors) because the accents were so *awful.*

His phone was in his jacket pocket, and he fished it out to check for texts that might have come in on the way home. Not that anyone would really text him—most of his friends were online, people he'd met through various art-sharing websites, and he'd left Maxi not twenty minutes before on the corner of Mill Street and Tannery Road.

Speaking of Maxi…he grinned, scrolling through his contacts, and sent a quick text once he'd checked. *Haha Maxi your plan failed!* He could afford to do it. Between classes was boring: the training rooms were off-limits due to, well, the class (duh…) and there was nobody in the lobby because, well, they were in the class (see previous parentheses). To top it off, that afternoon was the advanced class, which meant no lost newbies, friends dragged along to watch, or, really, anyone who'd not been coming to the same place for at least two years and therefore knew exactly where everything was.

Ergo, Tab wasn't needed. Ergo, he was going to spend the next twenty minutes or so taunting Maxi.

What plan?

Your plan to slip your bro's number into my phone :) I checked, no new contacts under suspiciously bland names!

Yeah? Check the number u have under 'maxi' ;) this is her 'bro', mate!

Tab thumped his forehead down on the desk, and felt a flush burning from his chest upwards. Great. Just fucking great. First the stupid traffic lights, and then the stupid bus, and then stupid Maxi, and now stupid work. And now stupid Maxi's stupid brother. *I am so sorry,* he replied, thanking the God of Textual Communications that he didn't actually know this guy, and it wasn't possible to sound as stupid by text as he could in person. Or be as embarrassed. *Your sister is sneakier than I gave her credit for.*

U should see the littlest sis. R u Tab then?

Yeah. You're Demi?

Only to Max, came the prompt reply. *Cos she's a sister and she sux. Want me to clip her round the ear for u?*

That'd be nice :) Tab agreed, and flushed a little. What was he doing? He'd never even met Maxi's brother. He'd seen one picture, and heard his name, and that was about it. He didn't go to Maxi's house often because of her disabled sister that didn't like strangers, and Maxi had never come here because in her worldly opinion, boxing gyms stank and were full of jarheads.

Will do when I next see her :) But btw, star wars is epic.

Tab raised his eyebrows. *You have a weird def. of epic,* he replied.

It's so shit it's good!!! U a trekkie or summat?

Meh, Tab answered. *If we're talking space, I preferred red dwarf tbh.*

MARRY ME. that was epic. scousers in space, u cant go wrong!

Tab laughed. Okay, so maybe Demi was nice. And had a similar love-hate relationship with the God of Luck as Tab, because you *had* to, to have a sister like Maxi, right? And he was kind of dorky. Which was nice, because art college dorks were into, like, anime and stuff. He hadn't really found many science-fiction and fantasy lovers there yet.

OK so maybe you are as dorky as me, he settled on.

Glad to be of service ;) Whats tab short for?

What's Demi short for? Tab countered.

Noooow i'm curio!! Oh shit, he was more like Maxi than she claimed. *is it initials or what?*

Yes, Tab settled on eventually (because it was true, his initials *were* T.A.B., and because there was no way he was divulging his first name to someone who knew Maxi). *What's demi mean?*

Mini, part, etc. like demigod ;) same first name as dad so maxi ran with it. she's named after mum too. stupid system of naming kids!

Tab had to agree, and said so.

Totes. Anyway tabby-cat, i must be going :) i gots me training 2 go 2.

What kind of training? Tab asked. He knew—vaguely—that Demi had some kind of job, but had never really asked Maxi much.

Army Reserves, running about getting muddy, all that nice manly stuff ;) plus my drill serge is fuckin hot but dont tell anyone!!!

Tab laughed, promised not to, and switched to text Maxi, but before he could get out anything more than *your brother is…*, Demi texted him again.

Good kitty ;) TTYL x

Tab scowled, and deleted that last one. He then scrolled through his old texts to find one he knew was from Maxi, and compare her unfavourably to a Wookiee.

Chapter 4

"COWARD," MAXI SAID.

"Shut up," Tab retorted.

They were perched on the low wall outside the main lecture block, Maxi luxuriously drawing on a cigarette in such a manner that it looked like she was giving head and having an orgasm at the same time. The way everyone was staring at her was *not* coincidental, and Tab hunched further into his coat, scowling. Even Maxi's cigarette was getting more of a love life than he was.

"You're a coward," Maxi repeated.

"I am not."

"You were supposed to have brought a picture by *last* week. Yvonne's going to kill you."

Tab shrugged. They were supposed to have brought photos of their subjects for approval, but he hadn't yet. And he wasn't worried about *Yvonne*, of all people. His 'development tutor' (whatever that meant) was actually an art history postgraduate student from the university, with the unlikely name of Yvonne Butterwick, and had that ugly-but-nice thing going on. Even though she was going to moan, he wasn't too worried.

"And if you can't work up the nerve to even get a photo of

this guy…"

"Nick."

Maxi rolled her eyes. "Whatever. How're you going to ask him if you can draw him?"

Tab shrugged, flushing. He'd meant to get a photo the other day. He'd taken a camera with him and everything. But then not only had Nick arrived with one of the other boxers, some pretty blonde girl had shown up towards the end of the class and waited for him. They'd hugged, and Tab had had a visitation from the God of Unwarranted, Unfair, and Unnecessary Violence. (He'd want to stab her in the face.) At least they hadn't *kissed*.

Stupid Nick. Stupid, straight, heterosexual, zero-on-the-Kinsey-scale, girl-hugging, skirt-chasing, hot as hell Nick.

"I'll get round to it," he mumbled.

"Uh-huh," Maxi said sceptically. "I'm just saying, you know, I am totally happy to ask him for you."

"Not a chance," Tab said.. His phone buzzed in his pocket and he fumbled for it. It was freezing, and he scowled at Maxi's porn-garette as she dragged on it again and the tip glowed obscenely. Her chest heaved, and her left breast nearly fell out of her clothes. "Slag," Tab told her.

"Jealous," Maxi retorted.

"Sad slapper."

"Lonely singleton."

"*Sllllllllllut,*" he said, dragging out the 'l' luxuriously.

"*Virgin,*" Maxi taunted, stubbing out the cigarette and jumping down. She was wearing a plunging V-neck black dress, despite the cold, and nearly punched herself in the face with her airbags of boobs.

"I'm not," Tab insisted, and she grinned up at him.

"You so are."

"I'm *not.*"

"You could always…"

"I don't want to hear it," he interrupted hastily. He jumped down to join her, and finally managed to look at his phone, trailing in her wake into the lecture theatre. *Hey tabby!* Tab scowled. Demi. And that stupid nickname. *FYI doom is on netflix and its epic so watch it.*

Too much shooting, not enough science, Tab replied.

Ahh but the science is terrible! ;)

Tab snorted with laughter, and Maxi leaned over to look. "Who's it?" she asked nosily.

"Demi."

"Say I said hi," she said, and grinned. "So you *do* like my brother."

Maxi says hi. "He's funny. And nice, unlike his twin sister. Doesn't mean I *like* him."

Tell maxi to clean up after she's done in the bathroom next time. she got mascara on the mirror!

"I did not," Maxi scoffed. "Anyway, I can do what I like in the bathroom." Tab dutifully relayed the message, and laughed, showing her the reply.

HOW DO U GET MASCARA ON A MIRROR WHAT WERE U DOING PRACTISING SNOGGING URSELF U VAIN TART???

"He's illiterate, poor thing," Maxi said sympathetically; Tab relayed that too, and was treated to a stream of abuse. "Tell him you're a catch."

She's trying to set us up, be warned, Tab said instead.

Cute as I'm sure u r, the bf might have a problem with that ;) Ignore her she tries setting me up with every bloke she finds!!

"His boyfriend's a knob," Maxi said ."Tell him…"

"I'm not a messenger," Tab said tartly. *Even the straight ones?* he asked Tab instead.

Once/twice yes!! U 2 @ college, then?

Sounds like an album, and yeah, Tab said..

U 2 @ College, by the And Yeahs ;) Get on with ur learning then, les artistes, and leave me to my vid games!!

"Dweeeeeb," Maxi opined severely, and huffed. "You're both freaks."

Tab ignored her. Maxi had just kind of adopted him—he was one of the few at the art college who hadn't come from Isambard High School across the road—but they didn't have a lot in common, when you got down to it. Still, whatever worked. *What vid games?* he asked Demi instead, transferring the phone to his lap

He just blates is and this girl met him from the gym once.

Ooooh, terrifying, Demi mocked. *U meet maxi @ college all the time. Just ask the guy and do it at the gym so then ur uncle can save u if he goes mental.*

Tab rolled his eyes. *No thank you,* he said. *I've had too many stupid crushes.*

Who hasn't? Dooooo iiiiit.

Why am I talking to you? You're unhelpful.

Hell if I know, u just started texting, came the equally unhelpful reply. *Wat do u no about him?*

Like nothing, Tab admitted.

Nothing? Just lust then fancy someone else!

Tab rolled his eyes, and put the phone aside, glaring at the useless ceiling. It was raining outside, he could hear it. He wondered what Nick did when he wasn't at the gym. He didn't even know how old Nick was, or what his last name was, or what his blonde girlfriend was called, or anything.

And he didn't want to.

Because if Nick became *real,* Tab would fall even further—and then finding out he was right and Demi was wrong and Nick was a) straight and b) hostile to creepy gay artists trying to take his picture, well…it would be awful. *Awful.*

"I hate you," Tab told the Supreme God, the God of Life Itself.

Thunder growled outside, but Tab was unrepentant.

Chapter 5

MONDAY AFTERNOONS WERE the quietest days at the gym by a very long way, with classes often cancelled due to a lack of participants, and Tab had been left to man the front desk in lieu of anything else to do. Uncle Eddie was in the weights room spotting one of the fighters, and there was literally nobody else around. Even the pigeons that liked to make feathery love on the roof had buggered (ooh, bad choice of words) off.

He was catching up on his comics. (And it was totally nothing to do with Nick's enquiry the week before, so shut up.) He'd gotten out of practice a little bit with the portraiture module, and there was something immensely satisfying about getting to use thick ink lines and forget about how realistic it looked. To be able to play with dimensions as *looking okay* as opposed to being wholly *accurate*. There was no way peanuts could balance like that anyway.

He was colouring his doodle—a peanut balancing drunkenly on the edge of a half-empty shot glass, wearing thick square glasses like Tab's and a little scruff of a brown wig that may or may not have been his own hair—and was wondering what to put in the speech bubble when a shadow fell over him, and a deep, slightly raspy voice said:

"The hell is that?"

Tab shrieked like a girl, and whipped the paper away. He then went red from his nipples to his forehead when Nick (because of course it was Nick, because the Gods of Love, Lust, and Not Looking Like A Prat In Front Of Your Crush never smiled on Tab, did they?) simply raised his eyebrows and waited.

"Um," Tab said.

"So?" Nick prodded, those sharp green eyes flicking down to the paper again. "What is it?"

"Um, a doodle, nothing," Tab said, shoving it under the key-board. "Um, there's no classes, er…"

"I'm just here for the bag room," Nick said.

Tab blinked.

"The sign-in sheet?" Nick prompted.

Tab went from a fetching cherry-red to a shade of purple that wouldn't have looked out of place in a flowerbed, and dived under the counter to get the sign-in sheet. He heard a muffled snicker, and pressed his forehead against the filing cabinet to cool the burning for a second. How could a fucking Monday go so wrong, seriously?! And *how* did it happen in front of Nick, of all people?!

Because it's Nick, of all people, the God of Honest Truths told him serenely. Tab hated it intensely for a satisfying five seconds.

And then he bobbed back up, and his drawing was in Nick's hand. Tab swallowed. "Um…"

"This is pretty good," Nick rumbled, turning the picture this way and that in surprisingly normal-looking hands, squinting at it slightly. Tab had never actually seen Nick's bare hands. He boxed in wraps or gloves, obviously, and he tended to wear leather gloves when he came and went. His hands didn't look as rough—or as big—as Tab had expected.

"It's, um, the peanut, it's drunk."

"Yeah?" Nick raised his eyebrows and eyed it again. "Should be on a pint glass, man. Nobody buys peanuts and shots. Trust me, I'm a bartender."

He held it out. Tab took it with a shaking hand. "Um. You, um. You like peanuts?" he asked, and flushed again. What kind of question was that? He ducked his head and pushed the handwritten sign-in sheet towards Nick, face burning. His blood pressure felt like it was doing something fairly dangerous.

"Nah," Nick signed with a jagged, tight script. "Allergic."

He pushed the pen and sheet back, and hefted his sports bag over his shoulder. Tab watched him—or more specifically, the back of his jeans—head for the changing rooms.

"Frankly," Nick yelled over his shoulder, "that peanut looks more suicidal than it does drunk, mate! Bring it back from the edge next time!"

The door clanged shut; Tab eyed his drawing, a little crumpled where Nick had held the edge between finger and thumb, and laid it down carefully.

It *was* a suicidal peanut, he decided, because it was falling for a guy who didn't even like peanuts. And to top it off, it was going to drown in the wrong drink.

"EDDIE, GERROUT," AUNT JuliKate said, the minute she'd whisked the plates away from the table that evening.

"Why?" Eddie asked, looking wounded.

"Me an' Tab are talking, shove off." She'd been with her voice coach earlier, and it was always dead weird because she got coarser, but her voice sounded more ladylike. Tab privately thought she was the weirdest woman ever.

"Girly chat?" Eddie said, guffawed, and then yelped when she slapped him around the side of the head.

"You're not a comedian, now gerrout," she snapped, and Eddie—Tab's *bear* of an uncle who had been a semi-professional boxer for nearly twenty years—knew when to retreat, and bowed out of the kitchen. JuliKate took Eddie's abandoned seat opposite Tab and plucked his tablet away.

"Hey!"

"You," she pointed a long finger in his face. She'd painted her nails. Blue. "You left your sketchpad out in the living room yesterday."

"So?" Tab said.

"So, I went and had a flick through it," she said briskly. "Saw your sketches of that lad in Eddie's intermediates."

Tab made a strangled sort of sound (he couldn't even lie to *himself* and claim it was a manly grunt, because it was more like a hamster being stepped on) and went a weird, sickly sort of greenish white. Aunt JuliKate rolled her eyes.

"I'm not fucking thick," she said. "I've known for ages you've been giving him the eye." Tab squashed the gross mental imagery that phrase produced before it could really get off the ground. "But now you've started drawing him, you need to get rid of this crush."

"Um. Why?"

"Because it's a bad idea," she said flatly.

Tab went from greenish white to a fetching shade of pink. "I've had worse," he protested.

"Which isn't a good defence," JuliKate said flatly. "That kid—Nick, is it?"

"Yeah."

"That Nick is a nice enough kid, I'm sure, but don't you go nursing a candle for him," JuliKate said briskly. "He's too much of a lad for the likes of you."

Tab bristled. "What's *that* meant to mean?"

"I mean, you are a highly-strung, creative kid who is not going to click with the kind of kid Nick is," JuliKate snapped. "You're best leaving this well enough alone."

"You don't know him," Tab protested feebly.

"Neither do you. And I *do* know you."

"Aunt J—Kate…"

"Don't 'Aunt Kate' me," she retorted, and Tab winced at the slightly shrill volume. Womanhood had not softened her in the slightest. "Take it from me, chasing after that kind of a boy is a bad idea and if you encourage your crush by this drawing lark, it'll break your heart in the end when he's *not interested.*"

Tab wanted to protest that Nick *might* be interested, but he didn't believe it for a minute, so he demanded, "What do you know?"

"Oh, please," JuliKate said tartly. "As if you're the only one. I spent *six years* carrying a torch for a man who wasn't interested. Six years. I knew from the beginning it wouldn't work but I nursed it anyway, and it doesn't *matter* if you think that…"

"Aunt *Kate*…"

"Shut it," she ordered gruffly. "You need to get a grip on this crush, Andy. Not encourage it. Why don't you find a nice boy at college, huh? Someone suitable. I've been there, and it's not pleasant when…"

Rant time. *Rant* time. Tab hated Aunt JuliKate's rants, and had no intention of listening. Unfortunately, she was impervious to most polite, mature forms of getting away from her, so…

So Tab resorted to his most childish—and most effective—method of drowning her out. He had begun when he was five and Eddie had been trying to persuade him to call Julian 'Uncle', and it had gotten even *more* efficient once Julian had started on the hormone therapy and slowly turned into Kate.

He put his hands over his ears, and shouted, *"LA-LA-LA-LA-LA!"* at the top of his lungs.

Aunt JuliKate snapped something at him—which he didn't hear—and stormed out, hands on hips in her fighting pose. He heard the bellowed, *"EDDIE!"* and took the opportunity to snatch back his tablet from her side of the table, dart around her in the kitchen doorway, and escape to his room. "Stop winding up your aunt!" Eddie roared back from the main bedroom, but Tab slammed the bolt home, wedged his desk chair behind the door and ignored them. Eddie wasn't really mad. If he was *really* mad, he'd have the door off its hinges and be bellowing in Tab's face instead. And frankly, even Uncle Eddie admitted that Aunt JuliKate could be tiring.

Tab threw himself onto his bed, and ruthlessly shut out Aunt JuliKate's warning. So *what* if Nick was never going to like him back? Tab could *watch*, right? That was harmless. Nobody minded him *watching*. Even Nick (mostly because he didn't know Tab was watching) didn't mind. It was *fine*.

My aunt just tried to talk to me about boys, he texted Demi, for lack of anything better to do. Unwisely, he'd left his art supplies in the living room. He propped his phone on his chest and eyed the recaptured tablet. Maybe he could do some brainstorming for this portraiture assignment. It was all very well saying he was going to draw Nick, but how was he going to do it? *How* was where the marks came from, after all.

His chest—or rather, the phone—buzzed. *Awkward,* Demi replied. Tab smiled faintly.

Yeah just a bit.

U out then?

Yeah, Tab replied, then blinked. Huh. Was Demi? Maxi obviously knew, but that didn't mean their parents knew, and Tab didn't really know whether the Joneses would be okay with that kind of thing. Mrs. Jones was nice enough, but he'd never met Mr. Jones. *Are you?* he added.

At home. I was out at skool—not my choice!!!—but kinda went back in the closet when i left :)

Tab frowned. *Sorry.*

Nah, s'cool. Easier—plus dont fancy tellin my drill serge y i constantly sass back ;)

Tab rolled his eyes. So. Like. Maxi. *You are just like your sister.*

LOW BLOW.

True.

Dick. Neway whatd ur aunt want if ur out?

She was telling me it's a shitty idea to fancy a boxer.

Depends if u plan on doing anything about it ;)

Not really, he'd kill me!

Then fancy away! Demi declared cheerfully, and Tab laughed.

It was dead weird, she's never tried giving me advice b4.

Aw, she probs means well, Demi opined. *Better than max giving u boy advice, trust me!!!*

She HATES ur b/f, Tab told him, grinning. He felt oddly comfortable with Demi, despite having never met him. He was a laugh. He *had* to be, really, to have survived being Maxi's twin all this time.

He hates her 2 so its cool ;) can b quite funny 2 watch actually!! I need 2 get u involved now, have a proper cat fight!

Oh shut up, Tab returned, and received a crying smiley. *Shut up!* he repeated.

Ur horrible 2 me. Defo maxi's friend!

Tab rolled his eyes, and called Demi a queen. He received a picture of a crown in return, so called him a fairy instead. Predictably, the next picture was of Tinkerbell. *Freak,* he settled on.

Yeah I'll accept that! Demi replied. *Like ur any better. Artists. Pft. What're you then, a science nerd?*

Duhhhhh!

Tab smirked. *Gonna go be a mad scientist?*

Not smart enough for that ;)

Tab rolled his eyes. Maxi said similar things, but she wasn't as dumb as she made herself out to be. Demi was probably the same. But then, he was in the Army Reserves, so maybe he really was that dumb. He couldn't have been in long—you needed to be eighteen, and Maxi had only turned eighteen last September—but Tab was convinced the military made you stupid by association.

The slow, marching death of moronity. That had a nice ring to it. He paused to note it down before replying with, *Gonna blow up enemy nations then?*

Blow em maybe ;)

Tab sniggered, without quite meaning to. Demi was definitely weird, but he supposed it was a nice kind of weird. The gods were being favourable with Demi, at least.

What r u doing, hiding from ur aunt? Demi asked in due course, when Tab had been quiet long enough. Tab suspected Demi was still playing video games.

Pretty much.

Bored?

Yes, Tab admitted.

Want some fun?

What kind of fun?

Got internet?

I don't do porn, Tab pointed out hastily. Well, he *did,* but not often, and he wasn't exactly going to be telling Demi about it. Or why he didn't do it often, because Demi would laugh at him. (Tab didn't like the lack of emotion in porn. Even Maxi found that girly and hilarious, so he wasn't about to tell her brother.)

Can't guarantee there's no porn, but—max's facebook password is i<3spnwincest. i have no idea what it means and i don't want to, but i've watched her log in enough times ;) Enjoy! x

Tab grinned broadly, dropped the phone, and reached for his tablet.

Chapter 6

"COME OUT TONIGHT," Maxi said on the bus home.

Tab usually walked home, but after their morning session they'd gone into the town centre, and then the weather had been Terribly British, What-Ho, and rained all over the place. (Maxi had said it was *'like cum from a whore's drawers'* because she was the crudest person Tab had ever met.) So they caught the X44 back out, and Maxi announced the veiled request (order) before the bus had even escaped the high street.

"Why?"

"Because me and Demi are going out—a pint and pool in *The Fox and Duck*—so you should come and check him out for yourself."

Tab reddened.

"You'll come," Maxi repeated firmly. "It'll be like a date. Kind of. I'll even fake a phone call after the first twenty minutes and leave you two alone."

"Your brother's got a *boyfriend.*"

"And he can do much better, and you're good-looking—don't pull that face, you are—and you'll just *click*. Across a crowded room and all that. So come out tonight."

Tab rolled his eyes; Maxi waved her phone at him, and repeated herself. "You suck," Tab told her, and sent off a silent prayer to a god—any god—who might be listening. *Save me from this madness!*

There was a squealing crunch, and the bus broke down.

Not like that, Tab grumbled, and whichever god it was—God of Engines or God of Combustibles, judging by the smoke pluming out of the back of the bus—said nothing. Of course. Sighing as one, the passengers disembarked into the rain, and Maxi slid her arm through Tab's as they started to walk the rest of the way.

"Come out," she wheedled. "Just the pub. Just you and me and Demi. It'll be fun. You never come out."

That much was true. Tab felt awkward around people. Which meant if he actually *met* Demi, he'd feel awkward. Really awkward, given what Maxi wanted to happen. Which would make it excruciating to go.

"Come on," Maxi wheedled. "He's lovely. You'll like him, promise. I did good in setting you up with texting, didn't I? You text all the time."

Tab made a grumbling noise. The sky echoed him, and he scowled at it. Right, yes, shut Maxi up now with some lightning and kill him in the process. *Thanks.* But—annoyingly—Maxi was right. He did text Demi frequently. Demi was funny and cheerful and they talked about TV a lot. (Demi fancied this actor called Karl Urban, and had introduced Tab to some TV show he'd been in, and Tab was still tired from catching up online.) And…and if not for Nick, maybe Tab would have done something about it by now. Given that Demi was just about the *only* crush (maybe-crush, but Tab didn't think it would be called that yet) that Tab knew in advance was gay.

But taken. Typical.

"Look," Maxi said, as they reached the crossroads where he went right to the gym, and she went left and walked down the canal path towards home. "Come out tonight. At least *meet* Demi before you write him off. You've said yourself you're not going to *actually* ask this guy at the gym out, so…why not ask Demi out instead and forget about the other guy?"

Tab chewed on the edge of his lip. She had a point, loathe as he was to admit it. Aunt JuliKate had had a point, loathe as he was to admit *that*. Nick was blatantly straight, and even if he wasn't, he wouldn't fancy Tab. He'd go for some similarly gorgeous, glass-cheekboned killing machine. As it was, Nick would have some dancer girlfriend lurking somewhere. That blonde girl who'd met him from the gym a while ago, she was probably a model or a dancer or a…a…dancer who modelled at the same time.

Tab sighed, and caved. "Fine," he said. "But just a couple of games. And it's not a date."

"It's a date," she said dismissively, and beamed. "Trust me!"

"No."

"*Truuuust* me," she sang, and let go of his arm. "Eight o'clock. I'll buy your booze, youngling."

"Shut up, just 'cause you're eighteen already…"

She beamed, blew him a kiss, and whirled away towards the towpath, those long curls flying behind her. Tab scowled at her back, then huffed and walked on to the gym. An evening out with Demi he could handle—maybe, if he didn't, you know, get an attack of The Nerves—but an evening out with Demi and Maxi with Maxi trying to set them up, and Demi would probably get awkward because he had a boyfriend anyway, and…

He texted Demi on the way to the gym—*Maxi's up to something, be warned*—but had gotten no reply by the time he turned into the stairwell up to the first floor. The door, with its printed sign, was ajar. A class was changing over, the beginners heading into the changing rooms and the intermediates loitering in the foyer. Tab wove his way behind the desk, smiling at the odd offered greeting, and dropped into the chair.

"Everybody in, ten laps warm-up to start!" Uncle Eddie bellowed, marching out of the training room. "Alright, kiddo?" he boomed at Tab, rummaging in the top drawer of the filing cabinet—his secret snack drawer in which he hid chocolate from JuliKate—and liberating a Mars Bar.

"Yeah."

"Up for a half-shift?"

"Yeah. Got some drawing practice to do."

Uncle Eddie ruffled his hair; Tab, for once, let him.

"Might be going out tonight. With Maxi."

"Right-o. Take the key off the hook in the kitchen and come up the fire exit stairs, or you'll set off the alarm in the yard."

Tab hummed, already flipping through his sketchbook. He was practising close-ups for the portrait. Drawing shadows and things. (They had shaved heads, but it was coincidence. *Coincidence.* Shut up.)

"Move yourself, Nick!" Eddie boomed, and Tab jumped, head snapping up. Nick had appeared in the changing room doorway, winding those long hand-wraps around his knuckles. They were scarlet. Much like Tab's face—and neck, and chest...

"Sir," Nick said, tying off the left hand and starting on the right. He nodded at Tab. "Alright, mate."

"Hi," Tab squeaked—it sounded a bit like a hamster being obliterated by a cannonball—and dived into his sketchpad, hiding his burning face behind the paper.

Because Nick was almost naked.

Tab had seen him like that before, but it didn't make it any less, um...nice. Of course, Nick boxed in...well, in boxing shorts. And hand-wraps. And nothing else. It was one of Uncle Eddie's rules. You had to apply for exemption—like some of the women were abuse victims and not comfortable being in their crop tops and shorts in front of the guys. And Nick wouldn't have an exemption.

Tab had just...not gotten used to it. And wasn't likely to.

Ever.

It being...Nick. With bare legs, shins backed by rock-hard calves. With bare arms, biceps like steel rope under the skin. With a bare *chest*, broader-shouldered than his T-shirts ever suggested, and not a shard of softness from the shadows of abs at the waist-band of his shorts—red as the hand-wraps—to the harsh pectoral muscles that formed under the cruel sweeps of his collarbones. Tab had guessed before that Nick was only seventeen or eighteen, but the body was finished: he had been lanky, perhaps, with those long limbs, but it had all dropped away.

Tab swallowed. Hard. He felt dizzy and flushed, and as the glass door clanged shut behind the oblivious Nick, Uncle Eddie snorted.

"Kids," he mumbled to himself, then threw the chocolate wrapper in the bin and followed his student.

Tab numbly sank back into the sketchpad, and flipped to a new page absently. His throat felt dry, and—as he always had when something had ruffled his feathers—he put pen to paper. Tab typically drew in pen, and now, rather than the tidy little edges of cartoons or comics, he drew the long, hard dashes of a physique. The sharp angles of bone. The harsh grate of stubble on scalp and jaw.

He drew Nick. He drew Nick through Tab's eyes, the feral beauty and unattainable charge in him—and it ached.

THE FIRST TAB knew of anything—of course—was when the glass door to the training room slammed back and Uncle Eddie barged into the foyer, his assistant instructor Marcus at his elbow, both holding up a couple of staggering students. The red was blood this time, and Tab scrambled out of his seat for the first-aid kit.

"Alright, lemme look," Marcus was saying, and Tab yanked the green box from under the counter before realising who they were: a ginger kid he vaguely recognised as Justin, one of the friendlier boys, and Nick. Nick was bleeding copiously from the nose, and his mouth guard had been removed by Marcus. Justin was muttering a rapid, *"Ow, ow, ow!"* as Uncle Eddie untied his glove and pulled it off.

"A&E for you," Uncle Eddie said flatly.

"Bloody *hurts!*" Justin said in a petulant whine, and Nick snorted wetly under the blood.

Uncle Eddie took the box from Tab, who hovered uncertainly until Marcus asked him for a wet cloth from the flat kitchen. He fetched, feeling weird and giddy and sick—because he felt oddly angry, seeing blood all over Nick's face like that, and he wanted to know what had *happened.*

When he came back with the cloth, Marcus had propped Nick up on a chair against the counter, and judging by the grimace on Nick's face, had set his nose again. "Hold the cloth there for him," he said briskly. "Give him ten minutes, give us a yell if he seems groggy or incoherent. Can't tell if Justin's concussed him."

"M'face busted his wrist," Nick mumbled, and grinned. He didn't look groggy, but he was swaying slightly and his pupils were huge circles of black. Tab awkwardly held the cloth against his nose, flinched when Nick hissed, and steadied him with a palm to that naked shoulder.

…Was it appropriate, Tab wondered then, to realise his hands were sweaty? Probably not.

"Um," he said, and Nick blinked up at him. "Um, are you okay?"

"Not the first time," Nick mumbled, and closed his eyes, frowning.

"What happened?"

"Justin punched me in the face without angling his wrist properly. Hit me right on the end of the nose."

Tab winced. It *sounded* painful, and it kind of looked it, and…maybe the bleeding was slowing down, though. Nick looked a bit white. Did he always look that white? Tab peered—and froze, like a conspiracy theorist in the glare of a UFO tractor beam, when Nick opened his eyes again.

He had never seen Nick's eyes *this* close before. And this close, they were like…woodland hills. Forests. A dizzying blur of brown and green and gold. A forest in high summer, autumn beginning to crisp the very *edges* of the leaves. Nick had the world in his eyes. The entirety of the south-west, or the Lake District, or the Peaks. Countryside. The German Black Forest, maybe.

How had Tab not *noticed* that before? He stared, caught by the yawning nation around a slowly shrinking pupil, contracting gently under the halogen lights on the foyer ceiling, and failed to remember to breathe for a good minute.

"What're you staring at?" Nick asked.

"Um."

"'Um?'"

Tab flushed a mottled sort of purple and managed to look away. Unfortunately, 'away' was roughly in the direction of Nick's crotch, so he found another away, and stared intently at Uncle Eddie and Marcus debating who was going to drive Justin and his swollen, probably fractured wrist over to the hospital.

"What about Nick?" he asked, and Marcus returned to shine a penlight into each of those insanely, stupidly coloured eyes.

"Feeling sick?"

"No."

"Feeling dizzy?"

"Not anymore."

"Black spots?"

"No."

"Stand up."

Nick did; thankfully, he did it without swaying, staggering, falling over, fainting, or bleeding anymore.

"Alright," Marcus said. "Five minutes, then wash off your face and go back in. No sparring, find a corner and shadow-box until one of us comes back."

"Yessir," Nick said, and gingerly removed the wet cloth. It dripped pink and he deposited it on the counter. "Thanks," he said to Tab, who made a sort of gurgling sound and wanted to die. Nick gave him a funny look before retreating, and Tab stood there like a useless zombie until Marcus lost the argument and had to take Justin to A&E.

Only Zombie Tab wasn't the least bit interested in Nick's *brain*.

"Put your eyes back in your head, kiddo," Eddie guffawed, and Tab recovered himself enough to throw the wet cloth at his uncle. As soon as the disruption had come, it had gone, and then the glass door clanged shut and Eddie's muffled voice was demanding something of the disturbed class.

Tab blinked at his sketchpad, and the black-and-white drawing—haphazard, but distinctive—of Nick. Of those wide shoulders and visible-but-subtle muscles. Of that wild beauty, that somehow looked sexier still in the aftermath of a clash.

He fumbled out his phone. *Can't come out tonight,* he told Maxi, and then switched it off so she couldn't persuade him otherwise. He couldn't. He just couldn't go out—not with Maxi intending to push him and Demi together—when he had Nick on the brain like that.

He switched pens, found one approaching the right colour, and began to ink in a pair of brown, green, golden eyes.

Chapter 7

SORRY FOR BAILING yesterday, Tab said.

It was Saturday, actually. Saturday morning usually meant helping Uncle Eddie decipher Aunt JuliKate's shopping lists while she was at her support group, and then going to visit Mum around lunchtime. If you could really call it visiting, as such. Sometimes they took the afternoon, too, if Eddie had bullied his assistant instructor Marcus into taking all of the classes, but Tab usually begged off after visiting Mum. It was too...draining.

So they'd gone shopping, and now were sitting opposite sides of a café table in Morrisons, so Uncle Eddie could read the paper and chomp his way through a fry-up, and Tab could text and pick at a plate of toast. (And, really, that neither of them had to listen to Aunt JuliKate fretting about going to her group. For all that the group helped her, she *really* didn't like going.)

You better be!!! Maxi told him hotly. Then: *Demi bailed too :(The bf called and he went running >:(HE NEEDS TO GET SHOT OF HIM HELP ME BREAK THEM UP.*

Tab ignored her—sensible thing to do, when Maxi was in a ranting sort of mood—and switched to Demi's number instead. *You bailed on Maxi too??*

Yep, came the equally prompt reply. *Sorry, but when ur bf has his rents house to himself 4 the nite…no offence, but better prospect than sis and sis's friend u've never met!*

Tab couldn't blame him on that score. *Maxi mad?* he asked.

Furious ;) U know what she thinks of the bf!

Why? Tab asked, forgetting to actually, you know, not just come out with stuff? And ask tactfully? And all that diplomatic shit? He hastily added, *U don't have to tell me obvs, I'm just curious.*

Lots of reasons, came the eventual reply. *IDK y she hated him on sight. Been 2gether 9 months ish. latest saga is he got really wasted and went home with some other guy. didnt techno cheat cos they just passed out drunk. i wasnt pleased but maxi went mental!*

Tab…could imagine that. Maxi was, um. Righteous. And interfering. Sometimes. But then…he'd go mental too, if a boyfriend did that to him. Any boyfriend. Going home with other guys wasn't okay!

Plus apparently he looks shifty. like max can talk ;)

Tab sniggered. *That* sounded like Maxi.

TBH dunno if we'll be together for much longer, things are getting kinda boring but its pretty good still. hes not out of the closet tho—another thing max hates!—so we have to keep kinda quiet.

Tab fidgeted with that piece of information. It hadn't ever really been a thing for him. The closet hadn't existed, because…well, everybody knew Tab was gay. People had been assuming since he was about eight. He just…was. (Uncle Eddie said it was the way he looked, but there was *nothing wrong* with taking time over your appearance!) And anyway, by the time Tab was, like, three, Uncle Eddie had split up with Jamie's mum and had shacked up with Julian. So it wasn't like Tab grew up in some gay-less void.

He couldn't really imagine Demi growing up closeted either—though mainly because the minute Maxi found anything out she'd broadcast it from the rooftops, and Maxi found out *everything*—but he couldn't quite justify it. He didn't know the family too well, and maybe Demi was only out at home because Maxi left him with no other option? It was a big and busy family. Secrets had to be hard to keep, right? They had two sets of twins—Demi and Maxi, and

Alice and Tammy, and Alice was like seriously disabled and stuff, so…he couldn't imagine Mr. and Mrs. Jones would freak about *The Gay.* They had bigger things to worry about. Like Alice.

But Tab wasn't thick. It wasn't like that for everyone.

Why? he repeated.

Y what?

Why is he in the closet?

Scared of how his friends and family would take it. IDK, I wouldn't want to tell some of his m8s either!

Tab snorted. Eddie rolled his eyes over the paper and said, "Who're you smirking at?"

"Demi."

"Who?"

"Maxi's brother."

"Bloody hell, that mouthy tart has a brother?"

"I told you about him. And don't call her a mouthy tart."

"Spade's a spade. Proper gobshite, that one."

"Eddie!"

"Poor brother," Uncle Eddie said emphatically, and vanished behind the headline again. *(WOMAN STABS HUSBAND OVER STOLEN KITKAT!)*

What's he called?

Judas.

Seriously???

No, not srsly ;) Moses.

Tab rolled his eyes. *Not Job?*

Ezekiel.

R u secretly a bible nut?

Religious nana ;) Ask Maxi for church stories when we were brats. Soooo much fun!!

Tab smiled faintly, and returned to the matter at hand. *U should stop Maxi tryin 2 set u up if u have a bf.*

U ever tried stopping maxi doing anything???

Point, Tab supposed. But still…*ur her brother.*

THAT MAKES IT HARDER :(

Tab sniggered; Eddie shook his paper and harrumphed at him

ineffectually. *Try harder!*

Not a chance, learned that the hard way! ;) Anyway shes not totes wrong. if i were single, id be gutted u bailed 2.

Tab flushed a little, and squeezed the phone in his hand, uncertain suddenly of what to say. Demi, like a mind-reader, helped him out.

Ur nice 2 talk 2, he continued. *2 many guys r boring 4 talk.*

Tab smiled a little wider. *Thanks,* he replied eventually. *Ur nicer than i expected. i thought u'd be crazy like maxi or just aloof or something.*

Defs crazy ;) IDK about aloof.

Dont think u could be with maxi about.

No, i mean i don't know what aloof means!

Tab blinked, startled. Demi's geekery made him seem…smart. At least kind of smart. He was into science fiction and stuff. He'd confessed the other day to owning the extended editions of all the *Lord of the Rings* and *The Hobbit* films. How did he not know what aloof meant?

Like distant.

Maxi's the crazy one, I'm the thicko ;) Tammy's where the good genes went!!!

How are u a big scifi fan and u dont know what aloof means? Tab demanded, then flushed red when he realised how rude that sounded. He started to type an apology, but Demi was faster.

Dont need to understand every inch of made-up stuff to escape :) Y i like it. 2 get away 4 a bit.

Get away from what?

Stuff.

What kind of stuff? Tab pushed, something niggling at the back of his mind.

Stuff-stuff. old stuff, new stuff. borrowed stuff, blue stuff…etc ;) all kinds of stuff. not important mostly.

"Put that away," Uncle Eddie grunted, folding his paper. "Best drop off Sarah's flowers anyway, eh?"

Tab paused, then switched the phone off entirely.

MUM WAS EDDIE'S older sister. By three years, but while Eddie looked nearly sixty now with his craggy face and bald head, Mum was permanently thirty in Tab's mind. Pretty, artistic, impossibly young. No matter what, that was the memory of her that Tab clung to.

She'd wanted to be a painter. Once upon a time, she'd just been Sarah Barnes and had wanted to be a painter and see the world. But she'd gone all experimental and stuff in college, apparently. Hung out with the wrong types. Not like bad types. They weren't *bad*. But they were all into drugs and weird philosophies and squatting and stuff. And it hadn't been how Sarah and Eddie were brought up.

Mum—or rather, Mum *now*—was why Eddie hated any and all narcotics. He didn't even let Tab have more than three pints in the flat. Because Mum had done all that stuff when she was young—booze, weed, the odd dabble in coke, then a bit of junk…

Then a bit more junk.

A lot more.

She sobered up, got off the stuff, went clean after Tab's grandpa died. That was before Tab was born. But she stayed into freedom and being anti-establishment and stuff. Fighting the system and all that. She still went out with the druggie-hippie types to random protests against Thatcher and milk-snatching and coal-mine-shutting and stuff like that. She danced around rocks at night. She claimed to be a witch for a bit, then a spiritualist, then a Buddhist, then nothing much at all.

She'd met a man at Glastonbury music festival, and then again at Stonehenge, and then again. They hadn't really been dating, and by the time Tab was born, the man had been long gone again and Mum had never spoken of him again. She just smiled and called him 'a beautiful spirit' and said nothing else. And then she'd been tied down to a council flat and a baby, and the wanderlust had smashed away at the walls and she'd been unable to *go* anywhere.

Tab didn't know—nobody really knew—if Mum had been a bit crazy before the drugs or not, but she was definitely crazy by the time he was four .He remembered being four and a half, and going next door to ask Mrs. Pemberton if she knew where PC

Thorpe was, 'cause Mum had locked herself in her room and was breaking things. Mrs. Pemberton had been horrified. PC Thorpe had just looked sad, and taken Tab round to Uncle Eddie's, and...

And that was the start.

She had good days. On her good days, Mum was fun, when Tab was little. They'd gone to the seaside or out into the country. She knew everything about nature. Tab could still name a ridiculous amount of random flowers you'd find in hedgerows and copses. On her good days, she was pretty and young again and loved the world and everyone in it. She'd been a good mum on her good days.

But she had bad days, too. Where she broke things and talked to people and wrote on the walls and hurt herself. By the time Tab was eleven, she talked to 'Josie' all the time, asked Josie for her opinion, set Josie a place at the table. When anyone tried to say Josie wasn't real, she'd get angry. Mum would, that is. Josie would, too, but Mum was real and angry, and Josie was fake and angry. She stopped seeing the therapist when Tab was twelve, because Josie didn't like it. The doctor tried pills, but Josie didn't like the pills, so Mum flushed them all away. She attacked Tab when he was fifteen with a pair of nail scissors, but then she'd started crying and tried to stab herself instead and he'd had to call the police. PC Thorpe had come. He'd given Tab a bar of chocolate at the station, and offered to drive him to Eddie's. There had been murmurings of a social worker, but she had never arrived.

It had been the beginning of the end. Less than a year later, Mum went into hospital for the last time. Adult social care had turned up. A few policemen had come. Mum had cried and begged and threatened, and then they'd taken her to hospital and Tab had been told to pack up his things.

He'd not seen Mum since.

She was still in hospital, and she wasn't Mum anymore.

He'd lived with Nana for a few months after that before Uncle Eddie offered him a job and a room at the gym. He liked it better—Nana called Mum crazy and said they should have sectioned her when Tab was a baby. Eddie never said anything. She was just Sarah. And from the gym, Tab could visit Mum easier, and Uncle

Eddie came with him most times, and…

And it wasn't so hard. It didn't feel so much like abandoning her. It felt more like…more like they were just waiting for her to get better. Like the hospital was going to make her better.

Uncle Eddie drove them up to the hospital with the flowers, but Tab asked to take them up by himself this time. Eddie shrugged, and Tab passed through the normal bits to the psychiatric unit, through the double-doors and into the sort-of foyer bit, where Jon, one of the day nurses, was sitting cross-legged on the floor with one of the patients, drawing.

"I got some flowers for Mum," Tab said.

"Okay," Jon said, and smiled. They all had the same smile here. "You okay on your own?"

"Yeah."

"You know she's had a bad night?"

"Yeah."

Jon nodded. Tab wandered into the nurses' room and filled a plastic vase. They were fake flowers, obviously, but Mum liked to see them in proper water. Sometimes, if she'd had a run of good days, they were allowed to bring real flowers. The nurses kept all the flowers and swapped them around, or gave them to other wards. Sometimes Mum didn't notice.

He put them outside the locked doors. Part of the psychiatric ward was out here, with the family rooms. For the more harmless. Mostly very old people who had had mental illnesses a very long time and nowhere else to go, or people who were mentally *and* physically disabled, but—again—with nowhere else to go. There'd been a man for ages who was convinced he was an angel, but he'd died a few months ago. He'd been nearly ninety.

Tab left the flowers on the table and hovered for a minute, like someone would come and say she was alright now. Mum moved between the locked and the unlocked bit. All the nurses called her Serenity—that's what she'd renamed herself, when Tab was eight—but the doctors called her Sarah. Tab didn't know what to call her anymore.

She was little and thin and wild these days. She'd gone. It was easier for Tab to think of her as gone, because…because the woman in the ward wasn't Mum. He could remember Mum giving him extra Sugar Puffs cereal on weekends as a little kid, and saying not to listen to Nana's grumbling because she was a nasty old bat, and helping him with his reading homework, and making up stories for him about all these gods and the little things they controlled, like videos and luck and rainy Sunday mornings. Even when she'd started to go crazy, she'd been Mum. Somewhere inside.

He couldn't see Mum anymore when he came to visit.

He'd been coming less and less.

"She's been doing well," Jon said from the floor. "The medication's working better now, and she's not putting up so much of a fight. She's started talking about getting out into sheltered housing."

Tab nodded. She wouldn't. Or if she did, it wouldn't last long.

"It's hard," he said eventually.

Jon half-smiled. "Yeah," he agreed, with the air of someone who knew beyond the confines of the uniform and the poor salary. "But don't let it shadow you. Live your own life, too."

"Still hard."

"It'll always be hard," Jon said. "But she's never forgotten about you, you know. Always talks about you. Forgets just about everyone else, but never you. She's dead proud, you know."

Tab swallowed against a lump in his throat, and Jon's smile gentled.

"She's never stopped loving her son, you know."

Tab nodded, asked him to take in the flowers before lunch so she'd know they tried to come by, and left.

There were none of Mum's—his—gods in hospital wards.

Chapter 8

"YO!"

Tab took a deep breath, tried and failed to keep his cheeks the normal colour instead of some bastard child of an illicit love affair between red and purple behind poor pink's back, and looked up from his sketchpad.

"Hi Nick."

Nick rolled his eyes—the eyes that had been dogging Tab ever since the broken nose—and rasped, "The enthusiasm. Rein it in, mate. Got the attendance list?"

Tab pointed a finger at the stack of paper waiting for the printer. "Uncle Eddie hasn't written a new one," he said. "Um, you'll have to start one fresh. Until the last gradings are done. Y'know."

Nick eyed him with narrowed green-gold-brown-*trademarkedbeautifulcolour* slits, and Tab flushed a little harder. "Uh-huh," Nick said, and settled leaning against the counter, arms folded. "You drawin' comics?"

"No," Tab said, and hiked the sketchbook a little closer to his chest protectively. It was his base sketch for the charcoal portrait, and he couldn't let Nick see it. It would give him away instantly. He'd spent too long getting Nick's profile—especially that blunt-

and-broken nose—just perfect, and Tab knew his own skill well enough to know the outlines would be recognisable.

"No peanuts?"

"No peanuts," Tab agreed, and blurted out: "You don't like them anyway," before his brain could apply a filter. He choked and the love child of purple and red promptly took a massive heroin overdose and went kind of bluish-purple, too.

"Seriously doubt your suicidal peanuts with wigs on are gonna give me anaphylaxis, but thanks for the heads up," Nick said, and propped his chin on his hand. "So what're you drawing today?"

"No," Tab insisted, pressing the pad to his chest.

"Walnuts?" Nick tried. "Popcorn? Space aliens? 'Toons of any kind?"

"No."

"Is it me?"

Tab's face caught fire, and his hair called the fire brigade and the police to cordon off the area. And maybe some of those hazmat guys to gather the forensic evidence for the case of *Nick v Atkinson-Barnes* in how Nick…um…Nick Boxer killed 'Tab' Atkinson-Barnes through passively-applied fire. Or something.

"Now I *have* to see," Nick said, grinning and reaching out.

"It's not you, God, don't be stupid!" Tab yelped, scuttling the chair backwards and clinging to the pad. Nick's fuzzy eyebrows nearly leapt off his face and gave chase, and it was just as well they didn't, because they could probably box, too.

"You," Nick said, very seriously, "are fucking weird, you know that?"

Tab scowled.

"Alright, alright, Jesus. Paper, then?" Nick leaned back, folding his arms and twisting to eye the newcomer who pushed the door open. "Alright, mate?"

"This the intermediate class?"

"Yeah. Who're you?"

"New," came the unhelpful reply. "Graded yesterday. Got an attendance sheet?" he snapped at Tab.

Tab scowled at him, too. He didn't mind being ignored, but

some of the beginners could be obnoxious. Like learning to box made you important or something. Please. Nick was, like, five times as good as this guy would ever be, and he called Aunt JuliKate 'ma'am.' Who'd this new guy think he was? He ripped a sheet out of the paper pack, viciously hoping Uncle Eddie would pair the new guy up with Nick and let Nick beat the crap out of his ugly face.

"Here," he said, slapping it down on the desk.

The new guy snorted. "Alright, faggot, don't get your knickers in a twist."

Tab stiffened; Nick leisurely finished his signature, pushed the newly-designated attendance sheet back towards Tab, and turned right into the new guy's personal space. "The fuck did you just say?" he asked lowly.

Nick had a voice. His normal voice—that deep, slightly raspy rumble—was sexy. But *this* voice made Tab break out in a cold sweat. *This* voice was a quiet, almost whispering voice, like a mocking lover with a pair of really big scissors and a serious case of the pissed off. *This* voice demanded a good explanation, and *this* voice promised that whether the explanation was good or not, something really, really bad was about to happen.

Tab dropped a hand below the desk and fumbled.

"I called him a faggot," the newcomer sneered, his chest rising and shoulders widening to meet Nick's aggressive stance. His lip curled upwards like a burning scroll. "You got a problem with me calling your *boyfriend* what he fucking is?"

Tab hit the alarm; Nick hit the newcomer. His arm lashed out like a striking cobra; the blow shimmered along his muscles, and the wet smack of his knuckles into the soft, much more malleable flesh of the newcomer's nose echoed like a towel slapped across damp tiles in the lobby.

"Nick!" Tab yelled, leaning over the desk as if to stop them, but the newcomer staggered and lashed back, and then Nick drove his shoulder up into a narrow chest and slammed the newcomer bodily into a wall.

"You wanna fucking *REPEAT THAT?!*" he shouted at the top of his lungs.

Uncle Eddie came crashing through the training room door, summoned by the alarm and probably by Nick's deafening volume, and collared both of them like squabbling schoolchildren, flinging them to arm's length. *"STOP IT!"* he bellowed, and Tab flinched away from the explosive roar.

The newcomer's nose was definitely broken, and dripping blood onto the carpet; a red mark was colouring the edge of Nick's left cheekbone, running around the bottom of his eye in a gentle sweep, and Tab curled his hands into fists, wanting to reach out and touch the injury somehow.

"Explain yourselves!" Uncle Eddie thundered. "NOW!"

The newcomer spat a gobbet of blood onto the floor; Nick shook off Uncle Eddie's enormous paw and fell back into a stance reminiscent of a soldier about to get a bollocking. Tab stared, and wondered if maybe Nick was a cadet, or his father was an officer, or…

"Newbie…"

"Allen," Uncle Eddie interrupted. He was still holding the newcomer by the collar, and the spade-sized hand Nick had shrugged off landed squarely on his shoulder again.

"…Allen," Nick amended slowly, in the same way other people referred to maggots, slugs in their picnic food, and mothers-in-law, "used the f-word."

"Fuck?" Uncle Eddie asked sceptically.

"The f-a word," Nick said.

"He called me a faggot," Tab piped up, and Uncle Eddie's face darkened. He turned his mass to the newcomer, who scowled at the opposite wall.

"Did you?"

"Might have done."

Uncle Eddie let go of Nick to march Allen the Newcomer to the door at the top of the entrance stairs. The door with the enormous sign in slightly less enormous black letters. "Can you *read?*"

"Yes."

"Can you read *that?*"

"Course I can fu—yes."

"Then you know the rules."

Allen said nothing.

"You break those rules, you're out. You call my nephew the f-word, and you're fucking out, my son. Your license is revoked, you're not welcome here, and I'll be putting a call in to your old man. Don't think Dave'll be too pleased to hear his brat got kicked out of a *third* gym, do you?"

Tab watched Nick, who hadn't moved, and was turned away from the reception desk anyway. Tab wanted to thank him, but Uncle Eddie was too angry to cross right now, and it might fuck things up for Nick. Fighting wasn't allowed outside of the training room. Brawling *definitely* wasn't, and Tab wasn't much of a boxing enthusiast, but he was pretty sure shouldering people into walls was against the rules, too. No walls in a ring, for one.

Once the door clanked shut behind Allen, Uncle Eddie marched back across the lobby and stopped three feet in front of Nick, folding his arms across his enormous chest. "You broke the rules, too, kid."

"Yes, sir."

"Which ones?"

"Brawling, sir. Fighting not for training purposes. Using violence to solve a problem, sir."

"You reckon you should be punished?"

"Yes, sir."

Uncle Eddie nodded, apparently mollified. "Bag room. You're off class training today. A hundred jabs, a hundred crosses, two hundred laps of the room. Repeat. You don't leave until I tell you to leave. Git."

Nick nodded, hefting his bag and disappearing into the changing rooms without further comment. Tab watched him go, chest aching for the disciplined power in him, hurting a little for the switch in temper and the speed of it—and swelling, too, because...

Because Nick didn't like the f-word. Nick thought it was wrong to use it.

So maybe Nick wasn't gay, but maybe he wasn't disgusted by people who were, either. Maybe he wouldn't murder Tab if he found out. Maybe. Maybe he wouldn't be horribly offended. He had to have guessed Tab *was* gay, everybody knew that, it was so obvious, but…but maybe he wouldn't be horrified that Tab liked him. Maybe.

"Okay, kid?" Uncle Eddie asked, clapping Tab on the shoulder.

"Yeah," Tab stared at the closing changing room door, and Uncle Eddie snorted, grinning and shaking his head.

"Nick's a good kid," he said.

"Yeah. Well."

"You could do worse."

Tab went pink.

"Kate's not the only one who's noticed," Uncle Eddie said.

Tab went red.

"Nor am I," Uncle Eddie said significantly, and winked at Tab. "But me and Kate disagree on this one."

"Uh…?"

"Want to get a move on, kiddo. Lad like that—well. Good kid, but he's a bit dense. Nice enough, but he's dumb, you hear me? You're going to need to tell him. Outright."

Tab flushed even harder—like, really, impossibly hard, proper scary red—and shook his head. "It won't happen," he said firmly, squaring his shoulders against the dream. "He's straight."

"Just sayin', kid," Uncle Eddie said, and patted his shoulder again. It was a bit like being punched, and Tab winced. "If Allen comes back, hit the alarm again. You did good."

Tab smiled, but never took his eyes off the changing room door, waiting. Even after Uncle Eddie returned to setting up for the one thirty class, he watched and waited, until the door swung open and Nick came out, tying off his glove with his teeth, bare feet oddly vulnerable on the foyer carpet.

"Thanks. For…" Tab called out lamely, and trailed off, tongue sticking to the roof of his mouth. He wanted to say more; he didn't know *what.*

Nick shrugged, and disappeared into the bagroom.

TAB FLOPPED BACK onto his bed, holding the phone above his head, and stared at the blank screen. It was half past eight, and he still couldn't get the way Nick had said, *"The fuck did you just say?"* out of his head. Nick had his own gods—the gods of violence, and anger, and justice. Proper gods. Not like Tab's gods. *Powerful* gods.

Tab wanted to tell someone. Wanted to spill it out, because this crush was getting out of hand now, getting worse, and yet...

This guy was a total prick at work today and got served :)

...and yet there was Demi, too. Funny, sweet Demi with the crazy sense of humour and the frankly horrible taste in science fiction (because *hello*, Stargate Atlantis was *not* better than the original, what the hell).

Tabby Cat uses bitchslap! Its super effective!

Tab cracked a smile, the heavy lump of lead in his chest dissolving. *Cats can't slap*, he said, and rolled over to prop the phone up on his pillow. He wondered what Demi looked like. What he was like *in person*. Maybe that would swing things for him, help him decide.

But then...Nick today...

Xcuse me while I apply cold water to burned area ;) you ok tho?

Yeah, Tab replied. *One of the guys who goes there stuck up for me and there was a row.*

Awww no bitchslap :(but I liked imagining u bitchslapping some1! No bitchslap.

Bitchslap next time??? Imagine i am making the biggest puppy eyes at u ever!! Slappings for girls! Tab objected.

Xcuse me, Mr Ur Sister's New Haircut Is Hideous. U R SO GAY. Also: EYES, PUPPY ONES.

Tab laughed, and tried to imagine a male Maxi making puppy eyes. Then stopped, because it was a bit weird, to be honest, like when he'd actually found some Batman/Joker fanfiction. Creep. Ee.

Why slap when I have knights in shining boxing shorts to punch people for me?

Too-shay, Mr. Cat. Was it a guy knight?

Yep.

A hot one? Also u imply nearly naked, I might need to switch gyms ;) Gorgeous one. And depends if you're good-looking, wouldn't recommend it if you're not :)

Couldn't possibly comment :P

Tab bit his lip, toying with the buttons for a moment. Too soon to ask? *Should* he ask? Demi had a boyfriend and everything, but he'd been a bit flirty sometimes, and…it couldn't hurt, right? It might be nice to be able to flirt, and have someone flirt back. Especially as Nick was never going to.

Well send me a picture and I'll comment ;)

Kinky :O 1 sec, kitty.

Tab rolled onto his back again, eyeing the ceiling and Jamie's constellations from when he was a kid. Tab barely remembered his cousin Jamie; he was more than ten years older than Tab, and shuttled between Eddie and his ex-wife after the divorce. And yet he was the closest thing Tab knew to siblings. He'd never know what it was like to be Demi or Maxi, not like that.

Did Nick have any brothers and sisters?

Here u go, Tabby! :)

Tab loaded the picture—and laughed, then scowled, then replied, *NOT WHAT I MEANT!*

It was a photo of a photo, and grainy photo at that. A school photo, of sixty or more teenagers in blue-and-yellow blazers. Tab recognised the blazers from old pictures of Maxi and her mates. The comprehensive on Grange Street. And all the faces too tiny to be picked out, and the name-plate at the bottom obscured.

Cheat! he insisted.

You didn't specify, genius ;) I'm in there! Third on the left, second row.

Tab squinted at the specified face, but it was just a pale smudge in rows upon rows of blue and yellow. Stupid Demi. He was white. Well that was helpful. Given that, oh, his *twin sister* was white, Tab had *kind of guessed that*.

Cheat cheat cheat.

:(I never cheated on you!

CHEEEEEEAT.

:'(Are u braking up with me?!?!

Yes, Tab said, *I'm breaking up with the invisible boyfriend I never met.* He flushed a little after sending it. Maybe that was *too* flirty.

Sign of madness, that ;) Gotta run, Tabby, Le Commitments De Four Nights A Week (le work) in ten mins and i'm late thanks to ur kinky little games ;) tally ho, old bean! x

Tab laughed, bit his lip at the kiss, told Demi he was a massive dork, and put the phone aside. Kind of ridiculously cute dorkiness versus…versus dangerous but drop-dead gorgeous knight in, um, shorts.

Chapter 9

U KNOW WHAT u should do.

Tab blinked at the new text, and shook his head. Like he was telepathic and could just transmit the *wtf?* to Demi that way. But he couldn't. Duh. So he texted it instead.

U should ask ur boxer out.

There's faster ways to kill myself, Tab proclaimed melodramatically, and could almost hear Demi laughing. He'd have Maxi's laugh, Tab imagined. That clacking, stuttery sort of laugh.

He wont kill u, he stuck up 4 u!

Doesn't mean he's gay or would ever go out with me, Tab pointed out.

It was a brilliantly sunny Wednesday morning. Cold, but sunny. There were no lectures on a Wednesday, but on Wednesday mornings the art rooms were quiet, and Tab had set himself up in a corner with a drawing board and his charcoals, to transfer the blurry imagined outline to a bigger sheet of paper. Maybe he could draw Nick secretly. On the sly, like. From memory.

He had a list of the techniques he was going to use anyway. Charcoal for the backdrop—black, to focus the eye on the boxer—and create that shimmery, blurry shadow effect. Thick wax for the actual outlines, in flesh colours, so that the image of him was firm even after Tab had blurred the motion out. He even knew the pose: in fighting stance, lashing out. (Nothing to do with the way Nick had looked as he'd hit Allen, obviously.) One hand up to defend his face, the other on the attack. Tab hadn't decided on gloves or handwraps yet, but they'd be red. He'd watercolour the red, to streak the colour off his hands, like he was moving too fast to see.

And if he could do it on the sly, Nick would never know. So all he had to do was sacrifice a goat or a small child or his Nintendo DS console to the Spirit of Secrecy, and all would be well.

Unfortunately, that didn't tend to go too well for Tab, so he was a *little* bit sceptical that this was, you know, going to work.

Never know until u try! came the cheerful reply. Tab rolled his eyes.

He'd kill me. With his face. He has a face that could kill people.

Only if u faint cos he's so hot all ur blood ended up in ur dick.

Tab choked with laughter, thankfully removing his stick of black charcoal before he could streak the design.

Ask him anyway, Demi persisted, with an air of finality. If someone could give such an air by text.

I choose life.

WUSS!

Tab rolled his eyes at the phone

Do it. Do it and not only will he snog u, I will, 2 ;)

Tab flushed a little. *Yeah right,* he replied eventually, without much idea of…

Which bit???

…which bit he was sceptical of.

He decided to ignore Demi's nearly-flirting (*was* it flirting? He'd repeatedly appealed to a few of his gods to tell him, but they were remarkably shitty at defining stuff, for members of a one-man polytheistic religion) for the moment and work, but it was hard. Demi's attention was…nice. More than nice. He was funny and understanding and kind of sweet, in a way Tab hadn't expected from Maxi's brother. Tab couldn't deny he *liked* the low-level flirting, if it even *was* flirting.

He just…yeah. Demi had a boyfriend, and Tab would *like* to, so…it was just a bit of fun. And right now he was supposed to be working on the portrait, not the fun. Even if the portrait was of a dream.

He returned to his sketches. It was preliminary—Tab worked in drafts, like a writer, creating multiple attempts before settling in for the final piece—and he was experimenting with the most realistic way to outline effectively a life-sized replication of a body. He tended to avoid portraiture. It was boring and…okay, so it was challenging, but there was no fun in it.

"Tab?"

The art room door clicked, and Tab glanced up. Yvonne Butterwick, his progress tutor, clicked across the tiles in her heels, smiling genially. Yvonne was always smiling genially. She was a genial person. She was a postgraduate student earning pennies at the college by supervising the students in portraiture and life drawing. Tab liked her well enough; he just…didn't like her subject. And felt kind of awkward, when she…

She trotted around the desk and looked at the preliminaries laid out across the table and on the board. "That's quite good," she said. "Who's your subject?"

"Guy I know," Tab mumbled.

"And what techniques have you decided on?"

"Mix."

She picked up one of the pages torn from his sketchpad. It was the eye he had drawn, weeks ago now, the day Nick had first talked to him. She studied it, then put it down. "Have you got a photograph of your subject, then? You'll need one, for the assessment sheet."

Tab hadn't even thought about the assessment sheet. "Yes," he lied.

"…Tab…"

"Yes," he insisted. He'd get one. Or…you know. He'd, um. 'Forget' the sheet. It would drop him ten marks, but it wasn't like he'd score highly in portraiture anyway. It was better than asking, and then being dead when Nick worked out why Tab wanted to draw him in the first place and killed him. With his face. And then buried the body or something. Right.

"You'll need a picture, Tab."

"I've *got* one. Just not on me. I like working from memory."

She hummed. "Tab…"

"I've got one," he insisted.

"You do have this boy's permission, don't you?"

"*Yes.*"

She eyed him. Yvonne was soft-spoken and soft-voiced, but she had a way of looking at him. Like she was a mum. Not *his* mum, obviously, but *a* mum. The *I know you're lying* face. He ignored her, very deliberately, and eyed the preliminary. He'd found the right pose. He labelled it with a tiny '*No. 1*' in the top left corner, and dropped it onto the left of the desk. Pose sorted. Now for the face. Nick's face would be a challenge, because it was all expression and sharp angles and hard lines. Cartoon faces were soft. Nick's *skin* probably wasn't soft, never mind his face.

Maybe his mouth was.

Tab shook off the treacherous thought and began with those piercing eyes. The colour would be the biggest challenge there, the *exact* way the green and brown blurred together, and the flecks of gold…

After a little while, Yvonne sighed and went to her own table with her portfolio from the university. Tab ignored her.

His phone buzzed maybe an hour later.

Just ask already! Dare you ;) x

JUST ASK ALREADY! Dare you ;) x

Tab just kept re-reading the text. He'd left the class sheet purposefully close to his elbow, and hopefully Nick would be early because he couldn't ask (about the *portrait,* not about a *date,* shut up) if there were loads of people, and if the gods could just leave him alone, just for *five* minutes, then…

"What's up with you?" Uncle Eddie asked as he passed through the lobby, energy bar in hand. Tab shrugged and carried on fidgeting. He needed a little luck right now—no, maybe, like, a ton of luck, like a luck *blessing,* and regretted not having made some kind of sacrifice.

What did the God of Luck like as sacrifices anyway?

The door downstairs boomed, and Tab hissed in a deep breath. He'd heard no car engine, but Nick sometimes seemed to get the bus and sometimes got dropped off and Tab thought maybe he didn't drive, so maybe…

Black boots clomped into view, and he clenched his fingers into the desk edge. "Hi," he squeaked.

"Alright?" Nick nodded, dropping his bag on the nearest chair and extracting a pen from his jacket pocket.

Just ask already! Dare you ;) x said the phone, for the millionth time since Demi had actually texted him.

"Um, can I, um, ask you something?" Tab blurted out, and the paper clip he'd been fidgeting with made a pinging sound and flew away around the room.

"Sure, if you don't chuck more stuff at me," Nick mumbled, scrawling his signature on the list.

"I…I have this art project."

"You have a load of those."

"Yes, but I have this particular one, as an assignment for portraiture…"

"For what?" Nick screwed up his face.

"Portraiture," Tab prompted. "You know. Portraits. Pictures of people."

"Oh, right."

"Well, I have to draw someone. And…I was hoping I could use you."

"What, draw me like one of your French girls and all that?"

Tab flushed hotly to the roots of his hair, and adjusted his glasses. "*No*," he insisted. "Of you *boxing*. So I can draw the *motion* and *speed* and things. There's huge marks for those technical challenges, and the lighting on a person actually *doing* something is completely different, and…"

"I get it, I get it," Nick said, and eyed him. "So what do you have in mind?"

"Um, well…you come into the bagroom a few times, like you

normally do, but…I'd just sit in the corner and draw you. I'd need to do a load of practice sketches first, and then take some pictures to do some of it at college, but mostly it would be live."

Nick shrugged. "Fine."

Tab blinked. "What?"

"I said fine. It's not like nobody's never taken a picture of me before," Nick shrugged. "You do it around my schedule, though, man. I can't go juggling stuff about."

"That's fine," Tab blurted out. "I mean…yeah, that's fine. I can do that."

"And I want paying."

"What?"

"Those peanut things you drew," Nick clarified. "They're right good, and you said you was into comics and shit, right?"

"Yeah."

"So I want some of them. Baby sister loves that kinda stuff, and it's her birthday in a couple of months and I don't know what she'd want so yeah. You give me a handful of them peanut comics, and I'll be your French girl. Deal?"

Tab flushed a little at the repeated reference, but adjusted his glasses again nervously and nodded. Comics. He could do comics. More peanuts on pint glasses, no problem.

"Deal," he said, when he found his tongue again from where it had fallen down the back of his mouth and right into his stomach, and Nick held out a gloved hand. Tab stared, then shook himself, and shook the hand. Even with the black leather between their skin, Tab *swore* he could feel a spark. His stomach melted. His guts flooded down through his legs and pooled on the floor. He wanted to dissolve, right there, and it would be *fine*.

"I'm not doing no naked posing, though," Nick said.

Tab went purple, and Nick laughed. He had a hoarse sort of laugh, like he was parched, and maybe it would have sounded weird on somebody else, but to Tab it was like…like…like the best sound ever. There was no other way to say it. And fuck it if that didn't make him sound pathetic.

"I'm kidding, chill out," Nick said, smirking. "You're dead

easy to fluster, you know that?"

"Um," Tab squeaked again.

"Why me anyway?"

Tab paled then, which wasn't something he usually did around Nick. "Um, you know, it's, um, technically challenging," he said, winging it frantically. The God of Totally Winging It, thankfully, was one of Tab's few benefactors. "It'd be really technically challenging, and I'd get points for that, and you're one of the nicer guys. You know. I figured, um, I *could* ask you."

"Cheers, I think," Nick said slowly. He was leaning fully on the counter, on his folded arms. He squinted at Tab for a moment, almost suspiciously, and Tab chewed on his lip.

"What?" he asked eventually.

"Nothing," Nick said slowly, then straightened up. "So, your drawing sessions. When are you wanting to do it? How?"

"Um, the bagroom. Like, you just…training. Whenever you can, it's totally up to you, so, um…"

"Friday mornings I'm always free. Got work in the evening, but can come in for ten."

"That'd be fine," Tab said, trying to keep his expression blank. Because, you know, there was the urge to scream or cheer or do something creepy like kiss him for agreeing. Friday morning, just him and Nick, in a ro-

Wait.

Just him and Nick.

In a room.

With nobody else, and the door closed.

Tab was the master of not showing on his face what was happening to the rest of him—when he concentrated, anyway—and it was just as well. His heart committed suicide. His libido did quite the opposite and threw a party, inviting his dick, his balls, and every ounce of lust he'd ever possessed as honoured guests. BYOMI: bring your own mental imagery. His stomach turned itself into an anxious ball of lead, his guts went on strike, and his rational brain retired entirely from the proceedings and decided it was better off taking a break to rest and relax before it had to come back and deal with the fallout.

Mainly, you know, the physical pain when he did something stupid In The Room On Their Own and Nick tried to murder him.

"Um," Tab said. "Yes. Friday morning. At ten. That'll be fine."

"Cool," Nick said, and raised his eyebrows. "You're seriously weird, mate."

You have no idea, one of Tab's gods piped up gleefully—but thankfully, Nick appeared to be an atheist, and didn't hear a word.

Chapter 10

THE BAGROOM WAS slightly smaller than the main training room, and filled with punchbags (duh…) of varying sizes and weights, hanging from the exposed rafters on chains as thick as Tab's thigh. It was used for bagwork (also duh) and the odd fitness class, but usually left empty for members to use on their own, so that Friday morning, Tab flipped the sign on the glass door over to 'in use' and set up a chair in the corner.

"Just, um…you know," he waved a hand. "Do your thing."

Nick rolled his eyes, still wrapping his hands. He'd arrived, bleary-eyed and yawning, just after nine, and had wordlessly signed in and vanished into the changing rooms, and Tab had been struck with the quite disturbing revelation that even grumpy and half-asleep, Nick was hot.

Which was going to make this session *so* much worse. Tab could feel a sweat rising on the back of his neck, half-cold with fear at being trapped in a room with a smirking boxer who would probably kill him if he knew what Tab thought about him, and half-hot because Nick was wearing hand-wraps and shorts and *nothing* else, and Tab could imagine the very little that was hidden.

And it was a *good* mental image.

"I'm just going to do some preliminary sketches," he said as Nick seemed to pick a bag and shift into stance. "I haven't done portraiture in a while, never mind, you know, someone *moving*, so…"

"What's the difference?" Nick asked flatly, and the sudden *bumph* of wrapped fist hitting the bag leather was loud in the echoing room.

"The techniques?" Tab suggested as a pattern of *bumph-bup, bumph-bup* started up. "I mean, it's totally different to landscape drawings, or blueprints, or cartoons. There's the line between making someone look realistic and making them look attractive, for a start."

"Cheers."

"Not that you need that," Tab said hastily, then went scarlet. Nick grinned, but didn't say anything. He was half-scowling at the bag, every muscle coiled towards the target. Tab stared at the curve of his bicep, shoulder, and back for a moment, then shook it off. *God*, his imagination for the sketches at college hadn't been anywhere *near* the reality. The gorgeous, dangerous, going-to-be-the-death-of-him reality. "You, er. You get what I mean."

"Not really," Nick said. "Not an artist."

"Um, so…what do you…you know, do?"

Nick snorted. "Me? I'm a barman. I don't do college or stuff like that. Not clever, me."

"You're not thick," Tab said hastily. He had his sharpest pencil flicking over the edge of the drawn bag, and slowly the blur of the gloves began to take shape, barely-there and flurried. *Motion*.

"How would you know?"

"I dunno," Tab admitted. "But you don't seem thick." He couldn't qualify *how*, but he knew that he *wasn't*.

"Nah, I'm not minded right for college and stuff," Nick said. The motions of the punches—left-right, right-left—were so fast that the red gloves were blurring in the air, never mind on the paper. *Charcoal*, Tab thought absently. *Charcoal for this, to blur the speeds*. Watercolour for the light still, but charcoal outlines instead of wax here.

A light sheen of sweat was beginning to rise up on Nick's closer arm. Tab noticed, and crushed the mental imagery of what else made him sweat like that.

"So what do you do when you're not…bar…manning?"

"Working."

"Yeah, and?"

"Also working. Boxing. Saving up."

"For what?"

"Stuff," Nick said unhelpfully. "Not a lot of money in my family, so most of it goes back to Mum to help out and stuff. I save the rest. Want a bunch of things—new bike, holiday, that kind of thing."

Tab bit his lip and swallowed. "Um, bike?"

"Yeah. Got my motorcycle license 'bout six months ago, but I inherited my cousin's bike and it's dead old."

Tab swallowed harder, the pencil flickering slightly. The image of Nick in biking leathers had risen up in the back of his mind, and he abandoned the glove-and-bag sketch and started on some harder, sharper lines. Stark definition for his back and waist. *Stillness.* A very slight twist around the hips, but otherwise…

"What kind of holiday?" he managed after a moment of banishing the leather images. Sort of.

"South America," Nick replied promptly. "Always wanted to go. Proper backpacking job, all the way round, like. I've got it all planned out, just need to find some way to pay for it."

"Well, good luck," Tab said, skirting the pencil around, brushing his fingers out from his still fist, to create a sketched cranium. It wasn't satisfactory, so he tried again. Skulls weren't perfectly round, and with Nick's hair shaved down, it was obvious. "Why do you shave your head?"

"I'm a doorman at *Sparkles*. Unofficially. Cash-in-hand type deal, you know? Anyway, it's easier if you look hard," Nick said.

"You *are* hard," Tab mumbled absently, then blinked. *Sparkles* was the gay bar in the next town over, and…"Unofficially?"

"Not licensed," Nick said. "I work the bar in there sometimes, too, when they can get the proper lot in. They just need a couple of blokes to look hard at the door and stop the local yobbos thinking it's a great idea to have a queer-bashing tonight."

Tab blinked, pausing in his attempts at Nick's crown.

"Does…I mean…do you get much trouble?"

"Nah. Broken teeth is a bit of a hint you can take a smack in the gob," Nick said, and grinned, showing off those teeth. "Plus a lot of straight birds come to *Sparkles,* not just the lesbians."

Tab hummed and nodded, giving up on the cranium and returning to the gloves as Nick began to speed up. This part would look best with charcoal edges, that was obvious. But what about the bag? Maybe he could mix the methods, change it up a little. Charcoal gloves and edges of the bag, but wax for most of the leather? That would give it the proper shine. And something sharper, better defined, for everything beyond the arm…

"Mind if I ask something?"

"What?" he murmured absently. Ideas were finally beginning to unfold in the back of his mind for this stupid assignment. He didn't have to do portraiture in the boring sense at all; the combination of techniques would be the big challenge, and then the added technical skill and better appearance would get him good marks even though he *hated* the assignment.

"Are you actually gay?"

Tab dropped his pencil; it bounced off the mats and he fumbled to pick it up, suddenly magenta. Holy shit. Holy *shit,* he'd asked, he actually asked, he *knew,* nobody asked if they didn't *know,* and why would *Nick* want to know, *fuck…*

"Chill out, man, Christ," Nick said.

"I, um, *why?"*

"Curious," Nick shrugged. "I know Allen called you that word, but I dunno if you're actually gay or not."

Magenta hit out-and-out purple. People always guessed. Always, always, always, and he should have *known* Nick would guess, should have *figured…*

"Don't have a coronary," Nick said, and laughed, the *bumph-bup* never pausing. "It's no big deal, I was just curious."

"Well, I am," Tab mumbled, nose nearly touching the paper. If only the God of *Death* could strike him now. Kill him. Kill him, kill him, kill him. *Especially* if Nick followed that up with *anything,* like, like…

Like why was Tab drawing *him?*

"Cool," Nick said, and Tab decided to breathe, the paper fluttering anxiously. Inhale. Exhale. Wait. Do it again.

And then…nothing. Nick said nothing else, the *bumph-bup, bumph-bup, bumph-bup* briefly aligning with Tab's heartbeat before his heart started to calm down, and it dropped below the furious speed of Nick's movements.

"You're really fit," he blurted out, and then distinctly heard the laughter from Mount Olympus, or—or the Empire State Building, or wherever they lived these days. "As in *exercise*. I mean…oh Jesus."

Nick laughed. "Thanks," he said. "Eddie wants me in the next interclub so I'm getting some proper intense training in first. I'll be grading soon, can't be losing before a grading."

"Like you've ever been a loser," Tab said, then had a minor heart attack. One of his demonic acolytes refused to do CPR on the basis that he put himself in that position, and Tab gurgled and went purple.

And then Nick just laughed again. "Trust me, mate, I've been called weirder shit outside *Sparkles*. Easily."

"Like what?" Tab mumbled into his knees.

"Like the bloke who tried to put his hands down my trousers to 'prove I wasn't a lesbian.'"

Tab's embarrassment was rattled. "You *what*? Seriously? Who had to figure out if *you* were a bloke?"

"Some drunk dude," Nick shrugged. "*Really* drunk. He was asked to leave a bit sharpish."

"God," Tab muttered, finally taking command of his body again and shading in around the edges of his best glove sketch. This would be a waist-up job, he decided, and focused to bring his heartbeat down. Focus on the *work*. Right. So. The very edge of the shorts right up, for a closer viewpoint. He'd only have so much room for the exhibition, and a life-sized Nick…

Morning. Earlier than this, like eight, if Nick could be persuaded. For the lighting. He'd have to get a few pictures in the morning, for the way the light streaked into the bagroom through the skylights. It'd have the best contrasts then.

He smudged the gloves with his fingertips, and smiled. *Bumph-bup, bumph-bup* indeed.

TALKED TO THE guy at the gym today :) Proper talked! And he didn't kill me or anything :)

Tab sent Demi the text as he dropped down off the bus outside the college, and was immediately hugged by Maxi, her bouncing boobs squashing against his chest. A guy locking his bike to the racks gave Tab a distinctly jealous look.

"Um, hello?" Tab offered.

"You have to make a move," she said, letting go and pointing a long finger into his face. "Seriously, like, right now, give me your phone."

"Nope," Tab said, tucking it into his coat hastily. She made another grab; he ducked away. "And make a move on what?"

"On Demi, duh!" she said.

"We're not…"

"I've seen you flirt!"

"Yeah, but it's just flirting and he's got a boyfriend and…"

"*And* he got dumped! Just now! Like literally an hour ago, maybe not even that, the dick just *texted* him out of nowhere and said it was over, so make your move, quick, before Demi goes and does something stupid like tries to talk the prick out of it or goes to see him in person or something!"

Tab's heart squeezed painfully, and he just blinked stupidly at her for a minute. The gods kindly retreated, figuring he had enough to deal with, because…because he felt bad for Demi, unless this (ex-)boyfriend really was a cheating prick, in which case he felt pleased for Demi, but bad about how Demi must be feeling, and then…then there was the selfish part of him, the part of him that kept Pascal's Wager and worshipped the gods to further his own ends, and *that* part of him…

That part of him was reeling in horror, actually, because suddenly Nick wasn't homophobic and Demi wasn't taken, and…and suddenly this wasn't a silly pipe dream, suddenly there was an edge of *possibility* about Demi—and even about Nick, if he hoped wildly enough—and…and…

And Tab didn't do decisions well. At all. Ever. Like, seriously, there was no God of Decision-Making here. Just Gods of Procrastination, Totally Winging It, Dithering and the Temple of Head-in-the-Sand.

Wasn't that just fucking typical. Minute in his life he got anywhere near two nice, funny, attractive (or totally stupidly hot) guys who didn't want to run away or beat him up for being A Homosexual, he had to *choose*. The decision wasn't made *for* him, *he* had to decide what to do *and he sucked at that shit!*

"Oh," he said.

He texted Demi with a *Maxi just told me about your bf, sorry :(Lemme know if I can help at all.* He left off any kisses, even if Demi used them a bit now. It would be weird.

He got no reply. And truth be told, Tab didn't want one. Because if Demi went on being his dorky, ridiculous, kind of weirdly attractive self…Tab didn't know what he was going to do anymore.

Chapter 11

THANKS.

Tab was distracted from Skyrim by his phone buzzing, and switched the game off entirely when he saw it was Demi. (He didn't self-analyse *that* decision too much, because Here Be Your Pathetic Neediness For A Kind of Attractive Dork Who Happens To Be Gay To Pay Attention To You...um, anyway.)

U ok? he asked hesitantly, retreating to the bed. It was quite late. He'd helped close and clean the gym, and now the flat was quiet. Eddie and JuliKate had gone out on a big date. Anniversary, Tab suspected, from JuliKate's chatting on the phone to her sister and her selection of something frankly *amazing* earrings to go with her dress, but Uncle Eddie was not the type to remember any kind of big date, so Tab couldn't be sure.

U got Skype chat or something?

Yeah, Tab said, and offered his email address. He reached for his tablet, and within a couple of minutes, a Hotmail address (*ddjones0209*) had requested a connection. *U ok?* he asked. He had no webcam (he was old-fashioned like that) and Demi made no attempt to activate one. Tab decided to let it slide. Maybe he was really upset.

DDJONES0209: Meh. Pretty pissed I got dumped by TEXT.

ADEQUATEHEROES: Seriously?

DDJONES0209: Yeah. Just 'I'm breaking up w/ u.' Thats it. IDK what I did and now he's ignoring me.

Tab bit his lip, Maxi's words coming back to him. To act before Demi tried to talk the boyfriend out of it and—oh, for God's sake, this was awkward.

ADEQUATEHEROES: What's his name?

DDJONES0209: ???

ADEQUATEHEROES: Your ex.

DDJONES0209:...Russell.

Tab bit his lip, and reached for his bedside table. He kept a notebook and set of pencils there, for the nights he couldn't sleep or he dreamed about Mum and woke up before dawn. He settled the paper on his knee, and printed the name at the top.

ADEQUATEHEROES: Whats he look like?

DDJONES0209: Y?

ADEQUATEHEROES: A game?

DDJONES0209: Weird kitty. K. Thin, bit lanky i guess, brown hair that he keeps cut short in the back but grows out 2 much to the front, blue eyes. long nose.

Tab sketched absently. Maxi had said he looked shifty, and he dumped funny, sweet people by text so he was obviously a tool, so Tab started with a long coat and a skinny frame. A bat with its wings drawn, but in the manky, damp way, not the cool Batman way. And he exaggerated the nose. Russell had a thin face, too, all pointy like. Like a weasel or a ferret or something. And floppy hair that made him look weak and slippery and sly.

DDJONES0209: Whatre u doing?

ADEQUATEHEROES: Gimme a sec.

Tab sketched hastily. He drew shadows under squinty eyes—too close together, naturally, for the shifty look—and a tight mouth. Because only a tight prick would dump Demi, and especially by text, and...

Tab paused when he realised how *angry* he was on Demi's behalf. He'd never even *met* Demi, but...but he was angry.

"Okay," he said to himself, and shaded hollowed cheeks and a long neck, almost spindly. The coat was grubby, he decided, and a dingy alley soon framed the creep. He amended the spelling of the name—*Rustle*—and took a photo on his phone.

ADEQUATEHEROES: Texted it :)

DDJONES0209: LOL! Thats pretty close, actually! Doesn't wear coats like that mind ;) He's a leather jacket kinda guy.

ADEQUATEHEROES: Well he's a creep if he dumps u so thats what he looks like now :)

DDJONES0209: Ur a god r u?

ADEQUATEHEROES: I know gods.

DDJONES0209: Have him smited then ;) Would win u brownie points with maxi too, she's furious.

Tab bit the inside of his cheek, thinking that 'furious' wasn't *quite* what she'd been earlier, but then Maxi obviously loved her brother to bits, so she was probably pissed if Rustle—er, Russell—had actually upset Demi.

Urgh, Russell. What a *name*.

ADEQUATEHEROES: Well she didnt like him but she doesnt like to see u upset either.

He took a while to type it out, going for kind-of-honest-but-kind-of-diplomatic. Maybe. Hopefully successfully.

DDJONES0209: I'm not like right gutted. I knew we were going to be over soon. just thort—

Thought, Tab guessed.

—he'd have more decency than 2 do it like that :(

Tab bit his lip. *Fuck him*, he said eloquently after a minute.

DDJONES0209: Not aloud now :(What u up 2 anyway?

ADEQUATEHEROES: Playing Skyrim.

DDJONES0209: SRSLY?!

Tab blinked, and scowled. Why did everybody *say* that? He was allowed to play computer games if he wanted!
Yes, he said, a little affronted.

DDJONES0209: Didnt take u 4 the gaming type. Marry me, 4 real. Skyrim, red dwarf, scifi, cute ;) ur the 1, marry me.

ADEQUATEHEROES: I will not be a rebound finance.

Tab informed him of that a little haughtily, but secretly was kind of pleased he'd obviously cheered Demi up a bit, too. He seemed to have Maxi's bounce.

DDJONES0209: Fiance?

ADEQUATEHEROES: That too.

DDJONES0209: what if I said I give good head?

Tab laughed, startled. Okay, maybe Demi bounced even faster than Maxi. But it was nice, because the silence all day had been a little weird, like something was missing.

ADEQUATEHEROES: I'll think about it ;) but only if u promise 2 not mope over rustle.

DDJONES0209: done. He never changes his mind. Once Im dumped, im dumped. Can I borrow ur fit gym guy?

ADEQUATEHEROES: nope.

DDJONES0209: puppy eyes?

ADEQUATEHEROES: nope.

DDJONES0209: head?

ADEQUATEHEROES: nope.

DDJONES0209: best head of ur life?

ADEQUATEHEROES: still nope.

DDJONES0209: y the username?

Tab blinked at the abrupt change of tone—it had come through without pause, and he'd been expecting another offer. But then, he supposed he didn't have much to go on from Demi himself to expect logic. Demi was all over the place, sometimes, just like his sister.

ADEQUATEHEROES: i used to draw superhero comics but superheroes are boring so they were more like adequate heroes instead. Like crappy powers and stuff.

DDJONES0209: did u make a proper story out of it?

ADEQUATEHEROES: not really just the idea and some drawings.

DDJONES0209: it sounds neat u should do it. what adequatepower would ur characters have?

ADEQUATEHEROES: idk, i had one with the ability to tell the colour of something in the dark, thats pretty useless.

DDJONES0209: that's pretty cool—idea that is!! U got any online?

ADEQUATEHEROES: no. don't like sharing it 2 much, it's not great.

DDJONES0209: that sketch of rustle was pretty good. N

u've got me spellin it wrong 2!

Tab privately thought Demi's spelling would have lead him that way without Tab's help, but he held his tongue and smiled, taking it for the compliment it was probably meant to be.

ADEQUATEHEROES: ur sweet.

DDJONES0209: thanks?

ADEQUATEHEROES: it's true. Ur really nice and sometimes ur funny. Sometimes ur jokes r just shit but sometimes their funny.

DDJONES0209: theyre always funny, STFU.

ADEQUATEHEROES: SOMETIMES. Anyway, ur nice :)

DDJONES0209: sometimes ;) but cheers.

ADEQUATEHEROES: u got facebook?

DDJONES0209: no, actually!

Tab was…sort of surprised (Maxi let him not have Facebook?) but also not, because Demi was easily dorky enough to not have one. Still…

ADEQUATEHEROES: why not?

DDJONES0209: 2 many keyboard warriors when I were at school. Gay boy with frizzy hair, u can imagine!

Tab could. Easily. Okay, maybe not the frizzy hair bit, but he'd been there for the gay boy at school thing. And he'd actually not had too bad a time of it, but it still was kind of unpleasant.

DDJONES0209: seen urs tho, maxi showed me ;) ur mum looks a right laugh!

Tab winced, sent back some abuse, and settled down into the warmth of the bed, drawing his feet up to his arse and resting the tablet on his thighs.

Tab smiled, and felt a warm coil of...*something* unravelling in his stomach.

TAB DIDN'T SEE Nick until the following Friday, when he showed up at quarter to ten with his kit and nodded towards the bagroom. He looked tired, circles ground in under those intense eyes, and somehow Nick yawning made a tiny crack appear in that armour. Made him seem a little more...

Human.

Which was the *last* thing Tab needed. Nick was already hot. He didn't need to be human, too!

"I didn't know if you were coming or not," Tab said, hastily rummaging under the counter for his things. He'd stashed them in hope, but Nick hadn't come to the first weekly class, and the second one had been cancelled due to a leak in the roof.

Nick shrugged. "Figured I can't slack off too much, especially not with the interclub fights coming up. Anyone else about?"

"No. No, Uncle Eddie's doing some private tuition all morning."

"Fair enough," Nick said, and shouldered through the bag room door. Tab stared stupidly for a minute, then dropped his gaze from the back of Nick's head to his arse. Not in jeans. In jogging bottoms.

He gathered up his papers, and followed.

"Are you alright?" he asked, closing the door behind him and turning the sign around. He chewed on his lip, then powered ahead. They were...sort of friends, right? They'd talked a little bit last time. Nick had asked if he was gay, so...they were...*kind of* friends. Yeah? "You seem a bit..."

"M'tired," Nick said, and yawned again. He dropped his bag by the chair Tab used, and unceremoniously stripped off his jacket and T-shirt. Tab froze for a brief second, then wriggled his toes and clenched his fists to stop his blood pooling in places it shouldn't (and places that *were not hidden well by these jeans, thank you very much, God of Aunt JuliKate Not Knowing Sizes!* Jesus).

"Why?" he asked, setting up the drawing table as Nick wrapped his hands. Having settled on the pose and techniques, Tab was starting on the final product, and yet his palms were still sweating at the sight of Nick without a shirt. He had the faintest trace of stubble around his jaw, and Tab surreptitiously took a deep breath as Nick turned away and took up stance opposite his chosen bag.

"Neighbours decided to have a domestic, cops were out, my old man got involved to tell 'em to shut up. Nightmare," he said, yawned again, and hit the bag. He didn't bother to warm up or stretch—and Tab knew if Uncle Eddie caught him he'd kill him—but the rhythm emerged almost instantaneously. *Bumph-bump, bumph-bump.* The bag rocked and shuddered contentedly.

"Um," Tab said. "Can I, um, take some pictures today? The light's better and it'd mean I could do more at college, and…"

"'Kay."

"Yeah?"

"Yeah, whatever." Nick gave him a sideways look, and Tab flushed, fumbling with his bag and the camera pouch. "Getting a bit bothered over there?"

"*No.*"

"Uh-huh."

Tab grimaced, and tried to waylay him with some other topic. "I heard Uncle Eddie say you're going to go for the first advanced grading in June."

"Yep," Nick said. "You going to swap your shifts around to say hi to me then, too?"

"No!" Tab insisted again, then reddened.

"You coming to the interclub?"

"Not for you," Tab insisted hotly, and Nick smirked. "I'm not! I'm coming because Uncle Eddie's saying I have to, give Aunt JuliKate some peace." Nick's eyebrow quirked at the nickname, and Tab's colouring deepened. "It's nothing," he finished loftily, "to do with you being there."

"*Sure* it's not."

"Whatever you're insinuating, you're wrong," Tab said primly, pacing around Nick on the mat and beginning to take some pictures. Some with flash, some without. For the motion blur. Nick ignored him. "Do you, you know. Fight?"

"Like…?"

"Like, you know. Professional boxing."

"Done a couple of interclubs before," Nick grunted. "Don't get to do amateur circuit until you're graded up to advanced here anyway. I will be, though."

Tab momentarily imagined him posed on the posters in the foyer, arms up in a slightly-too-open stance and wearing that sharp, *come on then you bastards!* face that he did so well, and banished the mental image. It was too bloody hot, for one.

"You'd be good," he said eventually.

Nick paused momentarily, and laughed. "You know nothing about this sport, do you?"

"I'm *trying* to be supportive," Tab said tartly, and his stomach shivered and flooded with heat at daring to tease, and getting no reaction bigger than a smirk.

"Try away, but you suck at it," Nick said.

Tab retreated with the camera.

"So," Nick said, in that conversational way that made all the alarms go off. *Warning! Warning! Line of conversation you're not going to like! Evacuate all personnel immediately!* "When does your boyfriend get a look-in if you spend all day behind the front desk drawing peanuts?"

Wow, Tab was just fucking *telepathic* today. He fought the blush, lost, and covered his face with both hands when Nick laughed.

"This is too easy."

"You're cruel," Tab informed him.

"Yeah, well. We talk about girls in training. Why not boys in bagwork? Equality and all that."

Tab huffed, and blew upwards into his fringe. "Well, there *isn't* a boyfriend. That's why I can spend all my time drawing. And it's not just peanuts." He sat down and picked up his lightest pencil. He had about half the outline of Nick's body, and needed to touch it up and finish it.

"Weird," Nick said. "I pictured you with some fluffy type at that college. Loads of 'em there, I'm told."

Tab swallowed and tried to focus—with difficulty—on the pencilled outline. A white silhouette. He would go over it in wax and watercolour and charcoal and pen at college, but the first layer had to be done with the live subject. Who was intent, apparently, on…on…

On finding him out.

A cold sweat broke out under Tab's arms.

"Re*lax*, seriously," Nick said, and Tab glanced up in time to see him roll his eyes. "You're wound up too tight. Need to get laid."

"So do you, it would work off some of that aggression." And he *did* seem aggressive. The bag was really getting it. The rhythm wasn't faster, but it was *harder*.

"Nah," Nick said. "That's a myth."

"What, are you celibate or something?"

Nick snorted, and grinned. "I *don't* think," he said tartly. "I *meant* the lack of agro. Doesn't calm me down anyway."

Tab blew out through his nose and pushed back against the…not panic, exactly, but weirdness. Definitely weirdness. Muse of Weird was splitting—like single-celled organisms did, that asexual reproduction thing—into two muses. Weird-Weird, and Kind-of-Nice-Weird. Because this was kind of nice, joking with Nick, but definitely weird because a) it was Nick, hard-as-brickwork Nick, and b) one word wrong and Tab would give himself away and get a punch in the face.

"Have you ever snogged a bloke?" he blurted out.

"Yeah."

Tab's pencil skittered. "Really?"

"Yeah," Nick said. "I work at *Sparkles*. I'm never short of a snog, male or female."

"Oh. Um. Any good ones?"

"Eh, nobody's that good when they're that drunk," Nick said.

He paused, catching the swinging bag between his gloves and steadying it. "Feel free to tell me to piss off."

"Um…"

"Why work here if you're gay?" Nick asked. "Isn't that like asking a straight bloke running a brothel never to fancy a go himself?"

Tab went *purple*. Berry-purple. So purple it was almost black. He could *feel* it. He felt nearly dizzy from the rush of blood, and there was a sudden pulse by his left eye that hadn't been there before. He was having a heart attack. Call 999, he was having a heart attack!

"*Oh,*" Nick said in a significant voice, and grinned very widely. He looked young and gleeful for a minute, and Tab desperately wanted to kiss him and strangle him. Maybe at the same time. "So you *do* fancy a go at someone."

"Shut up," Tab squeaked, bending over the outline determinedly. Finish. The outline. Then flee. Finish, flee. Finish, flee.

"Can I guess who?"

"*No.*"

"I'll guess anyway, your face'll tell me when I get it right."

"No!" Tab insisted.

"Just a warning, if it's that dev Jonathon, give it up, he's a right wanker."

Tab ignored him. Well, put on the show of ignoring him. In fact, he felt wholly tuned to Nick at that precise moment, listening to every inhale and exhale, listening to the shift of his feet on the plastic mats, and swearing he could hear the way Nick smiled.

After a minute, the *bumph-bump, bumph-bump* started up again, and Tab dared to breathe.

But when he next looked up, Nick was still smirking.

Chapter 12

NICK WAS ALREADY in the bagroom when Tab arrived from college, and Tab hovered in the doorway for a few minutes to watch before the rhythm slowed and he knew Nick had noticed.

"Hi," he said.

"You coming in or not, then?"

"Um, if it's okay," Tab said slowly. "I mean, if you don't want to today…"

Nick shrugged, and Tab inched into the room with his pad and stool. He hadn't seen Nick in a few days, and he stopped to gape halfway across the room. "I know," Nick said and grimaced.

His left eye, from that prominent cheekbone right up to the eyebrow, was solid black. The eye itself looked to be swollen shut, and Tab cringed at the sight of it. "Jesus," he said. "What *happened?*"

"I got punched in the face," Nick said. "Might look right authentic on your porter-thing, though, right?"

Tab winced. "Um, maybe, but…that looks painful. There's a first aid kit behind the counter, I'll just…"

"It's two days old already," Nick said.

"That's two days *old?*" Tab asked incredulously.

"Yeah. My head's stopped spinning," Nick said dryly. "You

drawing then or what?"

"Um," Tab said uncertainly, then decided he might as well. "If it's okay," he said one final time, and when Nick shrugged again, pulled the stool out from the corner. "What happened?" he repeated.

"I got in a fight," Nick said unhelpfully. "How's you?"

"Um, okay," Tab said. "Well, kind of. Sort of okay. It's stupid." He clamped his jaw shut, and wondered whether he ought to start devoting himself to some cult of self-discipline. There was some weirdo Christian group that like flogged themselves and wore barbed wire and stuff, wasn't there?

"What's stupid?"

That might stop him running off at the mouth, if he had barbed wire wrapped around his tongue.

"Oi!"

Tab jumped and flushed. Nick snorted, grinning that crooked, broken grin that made Tab's gut twist *just* like that, and resumed the rhythm.

"What's stupid?" Nick repeated.

"Oh. Um. It."

"Useful."

Tab arranged his sketchpad on his knees and sighed. "You won't want to hear about it."

"Why not?"

"It's about this guy."

"Fair enough," Nick said. "Try it anyway. If I puke on the mat, you're being too mushy."

Tab huffed. "I'm not *mushy.*"

"You totally fucking are, mate," Nick said. "You're that type. You've got it written all over your face."

Tab rolled his eyes and wished, futilely, that this crush would just die already because Nick was actually a totally acerbic, always-has-the-last-word tosspot sometimes, and Tab had had enough of tosspots. Even hot, nearly-naked ones.

"So what about this guy, then?" Nick persisted.

"You're a gossip," Tab mumbled.

"Yeah," Nick said. "I'm a barman. We hear all the good shit.

You know some bird called Karen Dawson?"

"No."

"Shame. She's had a bust-up with her bestie, and the bestie was drowning her sorrows in the bar last night and I know *everything* about Karen Dawson now. Need to find out who she is so I can blackmail her and fund my trek to South America."

Tab laughed unexpectedly, and the flutter that was almost always present when Nick turned up eased into a warm glow flooding his system. He felt too hot for a brief second, and blinked at the sketching table in near-confusion for a moment, the shadow of a boxer almost seeming to move.

"There's this guy," he blurted out.

"Uh-huh."

"I've never actually met him," Tab said. "We text. His sister tried to set us up and he was really nice about it and he's just…dead funny and sweet and I like him."

"So what's the problem?" Nick rasped, focusing on the bag. There was a light sheen of sweat beginning to build on his shoulders, but he didn't seem so angry as he had when Tab had arrived. Not quite so…brutal, perhaps.

"I like someone else, too."

"Ahh," Nick said, and paused, clasping the bag between both gloves to steady it. His eyes were a fierce colour, and Tab wondered how to capture them. Perhaps a more textured approach? Or even a different medium altogether, like broken glass or something like it stuck to the paper? A patchwork boxer. "So you don't know who to go for?"

"No," Tab admitted.

"Well, what's the other guy like?"

"Straight," Tab blurted out.

"Ouch," Nick said.

"Mm. And really, really hot. Like…*really* hot. This other guy, the phone guy—Demi—has anyone called Demi ever come into your bar?"

"Demi?" Nick echoed, and frowned. "Uh. Demi?"

"Yeah."

"…Not that I know of, no. Uh. No. Weird name."

"Well, Demi's sweet and funny and everything, but he's not *hot* like this other guy, and…"

"Never," Nick said firmly, "go for the hot guy."

Tab blinked, pausing in his work. He was using pointillism—the dot method—for Nick's hips and waist, because they stayed quite still when he used the bags, and Tab simply stopped in the middle of outlining the waistband of Nick's shorts in those tiny, exact black dots.

"Why?" he asked, blinking. Nick couldn't know, he decided. The Spirits of Privacy and Decorum had been kind to him and kept Nick in the grasp of the Muse of Ignorance. Nick couldn't know, because if he did, he would tell Tab to go for the hot one, and then kill him for thinking Nick was hot.

"Because the hot one is never worth it," Nick shrugged. "Trust me, I've been there. It's great for a quick fling, but if you're agonising over it, you're not up for a quick fling, are you?"

"Well, no, I…"

"And hot people are either fucking nasty, or fucking thick," Nick said, and grinned. "And if *I* can say someone's thick, they're *thick.*"

"You're not thick," Tab protested.

"Yeah I am," Nick said. "I have like six GCSEs. And the best one is a C."

"In what?"

Nick grimaced.

"In what?" Tab persisted. "What did you get the C in?"

"German," Nick said finally, and rolled his eyes. "I hated school."

"I…can see that," Tab admitted. "You don't seem like the type who'd…"

"Nah," Nick interrupted. "I was bullied."

Tab blinked. "Seriously?"

"Yep."

"…*Bullied.* You?"

"Yep."

"…How?!" Tab yelped, and went promptly magenta. "Sorry. Sorry! I mean—I mean it seems weird, anyone bullying you, I mean, you're like really tough and…"

"And, I'm really not, it's an image," Nick said flatly. "I got bullied out of six schools by the time I was thirteen. I dropped out at fifteen, to be honest. I didn't even go to most of my exams."

"Shit," Tab breathed.

Nick shrugged and resumed the fighting stance. "It's cool," he said. "I got out of there, got a job, took up boxing. People don't argue anymore."

"No shit," Tab blurted out, and groaned. "I am digging such a hole."

"Eh, I don't think you've stopped digging since I first said hi," Nick said. "So anyway. These dudes you like. Go for the nice guy, because that might *actually* be a decent thing."

Tab bit his lip, returning to his dots, and thought that Nick really was the hottest bastard in the world. Because…because he wasn't just a hot guy, was he? He was nice, too. He was…he had a history. He had a history Tab had never imagined. He wasn't just this hard-as-stone facade, he was…someone else, too.

Nick wasn't what Tab had imagined…and it was only clouding the issue.

THE SKETCHING ROOM was quiet when Tab arrived the following morning. It was only half-full, as these sessions weren't mandatory unless it was your turn to show Yvonne your progress, but that wasn't why the quiet was so strange.

It was because Maxi was there, and it was quiet.

"What's up?" Tab asked lowly as he took up the drawing board beside hers and unrolled his paper, clipping it into place with loud snaps.

She shook her head. She looked morose, her eyes rimmed in red that was natural for once, and her entire posture screaming despondency, from the slouch in her shoulders to the limp grip she had on her pencil. She had decided eventually on the elegant black-and-white approach, the entire portrait being drawn in little, stunted flicks as opposed to long and continuous lines. Tab couldn't remember what the flicks were representing about Alice.

"Max?" he prompted, once he was set up and she'd still said nothing.

She glanced over her shoulder at Yvonne, the weight of her curls dragging across her back and seeming less lively than usual, before finally speaking. "Alice is back in hospital."

"Oh," Tab said.

"She's got pneumonia."

"Oh," he repeated uselessly.

"They've put her in a coma," Maxi said dully, "until it clears up. Only the doctor said if. 'Cause she's really, really sick this time."

To Tab's horror, she put down her pencil and began to cry. Maxi didn't cry—in fact, Tab had never seen her cry at all—but suddenly she was heaving great sobs, and an ugly redness was blooming across her face.

Tab went on autopilot—Mum had cried a lot, before—and didn't even look at Yvonne, putting an arm around Maxi's heaving shoulders and guiding her out of the sketching room and into the ladies toilets. Who cared if he wasn't meant to be here—he was gay, it was totally fine. He handed her a wad of toilet paper for her nose, and tried not to think about the state of his shirt when she wrapped around him in a hug and wailed into his shoulder.

He petted her hair instead. She had very springy curls, and they were kind of fun to play with. So he played with them, and made all the right noises, and waited it out. Tab didn't like crying people. It made him feel awkward and embarrassed. Mum had cried lots when he was little, and he always felt weird about it because she was *Mum* and she was fighting Capitalism and Conservatory Parties (later, he had discovered, the *Conservative* Party) and The Establishment and why was she crying? And it had stuck with him. Crying was weird and awkward.

Thankfully, though, Maxi was an evil villainess and didn't cry long. She snuffled and blew her nose horribly loudly into the toilet paper and then turned her attention to the mirror and trying to get all the smudgy mascara off.

"Sorry," she mumbled. "It's just, you know. They've never put her in a coma before."

"It's okay," he mumbled.

"And I feel really crappy because I was out with Josh Felton—you know, ginger Josh, from the drama department—I went out with him yesterday and then Mum had to take Alice to hospital and Demi stayed up with Alice until like two in the morning when they put her under and he was shattered when he got home and Demi's never shattered, and…"

She sniffled dangerously, and Tab patted her arm. "Um," he said. "I'm sure it's just a precaution. To like, let her rest and focus on getting better and stuff. Right?"

"Mm, maybe," she snorted unpleasantly, and Tab wrinkled his nose. "Oh shut up, I'm allowed to be ugly when I'm upset."

"We-ell…"

"Not a word," she warned dangerously, and Tab cracked a smile. That was better. Maxi being prickly was way better than Maxi in tears.

"I'm sure she'll be okay," he repeated uselessly.

"Yeah. Sorry. Yeah," Maxi repeated, and squared her shoulders. "She's a *Jones*, right. And we're tough."

"Barmy."

"Same thing," she sniped. "Sorry. 'Bout your shirt."

"Don't worry about it. Is Demi okay?"

"I don't know, probably," she rolled her eyes. "He turned into a right *boy* last year, he just grunts at me these days. He was asleep when I left this morning anyway. I'll text him later. He'll probably go back to the hospital, he's Alice's favourite, 'cause he does all the nerdy voices out of her picture books for her. He'll go read to her. Do you think she'll hear him?"

"Maybe," Tab hedged. "I saw a programme once that said unconscious people can hear you."

"I hope she hears him, she's scared of hospital," Maxi mumbled.

"She'll be fine," Tab offered weakly.

"Yeah," Maxi mumbled, and sighed heavily. "C'mon. Let's go back in. I haven't seen your portrait yet."

"It's just an outline."

"When are you going to add the face?"

"Last. I hate faces."

She pouted, but Tab would not be moved, and Yvonne just nodded at them when they slipped back into the sketching room. Maxi ended up only picking over her own work, and spent most of it suggesting—for once, *good* suggestions too—how to improve Tab's medley of methods.

He texted Demi when Yvonne wasn't looking—a quick and simple, *heard about alice, u ok?*—but got no reply.

Chapter 13

By the afternoon, Demi still hadn't given any kind of an answer, and Tab decided to leave him alone. Maxi didn't cry, so this had to be kind of a big deal, and maybe he wasn't even allowed his phone on where Alice was in the hospital?

The gym was quiet when he arrived. The intermediate class had already started, so Tab set himself up behind the reception desk with his tablet and sketchpad and began to draw, of all things, more peanuts. (For practice, he told himself, but there was no lying to the gods. A God of Nick was being formed. Maybe even Nick himself was a God.)

He was halfway through the first page of the comic when the door opened, and it was so unusual—nobody arrived halfway through a class, they were *far* too early for the next one—that he paused and looked up.

"Hi," said the girl.

"Er," Tab said. "Hi? Can I help?"

She wasn't a boxer. There *were* women who boxed here—there was even an all-women class on Sundays—but this girl wasn't one of them. She was Tab's age, and tiny and very blonde. She'd be more suited to ballet than boxing, and looked very faintly familiar, as though Tab had seen her around, but only once or twice.

"Can I wait in here?" she asked. "I'm waiting for Nick? In the intermediate class? He said you wouldn't mind if I waited up here. And it's absolutely slating outside." Well, yes. It had been raining all day. Tab hadn't dared bring his portrait back from college because of it. "Um," she added, "I can wait downstairs for him if you'd prefer."

Tab felt sick, but jolted at the add-on. "No," he said. "Um, sorry. No, you can wait here. S'fine." He gestured with his pen at the squashy sofas alongside the desk, and she beamed. He felt even sicker. She was very, very pretty. Stupidly pretty, in fact. Stupidly, offensively, obnoxiously, horribly, infuriatingly pretty.

"Oh, are you drawing?" she asked, dropping her bag on one of the sofas and wandering over. "Nick said you were an artist."

From anyone else, Tab might have fainted at the idea Nick talked about him, but from this bimbo, he was just angry. *Go away,* he thought in her direction as loudly as possible. *Emigrate to China and don't come back.*

"That's dead good," she enthused, peering at the comic upside-down, and then grinned at Tab. She had very blue eyes, big and round. "Between you and me, I think it's good Nick's noticed your work, you know. He's not very into art." She rolled her eyes. "I've been trying to sweet-talk him into coming to the ballet..." *Bingo!* "...with me for *ages,* but he won't do it."

"I'm not really into dance," Tab said.

"Boxing's just dancing for men."

"Well, there's a lot of beating each other up, too," Tab said flatly, but she only giggled. He squeezed his pen so hard it creaked. *GO AWAY.*

"I'm Luce," she said.

"Tab."

"Tab. That's an interesting name." She paused, but he refused to take the cue and elaborate. "Nick didn't actually know your name, you know." Tab flushed hotly. "He's got a really bad memory, ignore him. He still calls me Stella occasionally—I drink Stella at the pub, hence, you know—but he forgets *my* name and me and Nick have been a thing for ages…"

Tab wanted to hurl. Instead, he very calmly put down his pen and said, "'Scuse me. I have to check the equipment at two." Lies.

He disappeared into the bagroom and shut the door behind him to keep *Luce* in the foyer. When he heard the glass door to the training area clang a while later, he stayed where he was, piling up the floor mats that needed re-stitching or re-stuffing, and tried to quell the burning rage in his face and the bitter, *sour* disappointment in his stomach.

Stupid Luce and her ballet and blonde hair and being Nick's girlfriend. Stupid Nick and his straightness and thing for pretty girls and being a *nice guy* under the hard exterior. And stupid Tab, for ever falling for a straight guy in the first place.

The peanut wasn't just suicidal, it was downright *mad*.

IT'S FINE. U ok?

Tab blinked at his phone before picking it up and reading the text properly. Demi. It was half past nine, but Demi had finally surfaced from looking after Alice at the hospital, and had just said…

I'm okay, Tab replied. *Are u and Maxi?*

Yeah, came the prompt reply. *Ally's doing better now. And I got to sleep! :)*

Tab smiled faintly. *U feeling better then?*

Mm, defs. Hows u then?

Disappointed, Tab said honestly. *The boxer's girlfriend came to the gym today.*

Urrrrgh :(Nooooo. Was she stunning and gorgeous and had tits you could set a table on?

Yeah.

Won't last, it's just sex and a bit of rough, chase the harpy away and grab ur man! :D

And horribly embarrass myself in the meantime, no way, Tab replied, but sniggered anyway at the mental image. Maybe he could draw that and pass it to Maxi to give to Demi. *The Adventures of Harry the*

Harpy-Chaser. That would be pretty freaky, and it would probably cheer Demi up a bit, too.

Aww, but that's half the fun of dating ;) Ah well better luck next time. U never no, maybe ur like Captain Kirk and everyone u ever go for will be killed in a freak accident before the end of the day :O

Or maybe not?

Yeah, maybe more like Sulu.

Dick, Tab replied flatly, and shuddered. Ew. Seriously, no actor ever before about 1995 had been hot. Especially not anybody off *Star Trek.*

Yes, that is a central part of being flaaaaaaaamiiiiiing :D

R U DRUNK??? Tab demanded.

Nope.

I don't often say this, Tab stated, *but Maxi's right. Ur a dweeb.*

He flushed hotly when Demi replied, *Yeah but u love it, tabby-cat ;)* Because the dick (and he *was* a dick, because he was Maxi's brother and was cut from the same dickish cloth and was being a dick a genetic trait because *it so totally ran in that family*) was kind of totally horribly *right*, and that made him a dick.

Dick, Tab repeated.

:'(Cruel. Ur an android or something, u have no heart. Like the guy out of Wizz of Oz.

That was the lion.

The tin man, ACTUALLY, so my point is doubly valid :D Anyway I know u have a heart—flirt. Ooh, a heartflirt. U have a heartflirt.

I do not flirt.

Yeah u totes do. U just don't know u do. I quote, ur text last week on tues at half 8, u ended it with 3 kisses.

I did not, Tab denied, even as he knew he had. He felt himself flushing, even though Demi couldn't see him.

U did. Xxx. Like that. Xxx

And now u just sent me 6 kisses so whose flirting now???

*Who's.

Grammar kink?

Totes ;) Demi replied, and Tab flushed. *Bet u've got looooads of kinks.*

Couldn't possibly comment, Tab parroted.

Well-played, good sir. But 4 srs, bet u do. BET. U. DO.

I wouldn't know, I'm not a whore like u and Maxi ;)

Oooh, burn, Demi taunted. *U'd love to explore my kinks.*

Tab flushed again, but…differently. Not so intensely. And he felt weirdly…uncomfortable and not. Like Demi had said something embarrassing but…

But, the God of Horribly Honest Truths—who was Tab's long-term sponsor—murmured, *not untrue.*

Depends what they are, Tab said boldly.

Wahey ;) U'll have to find out.

Well gimme some hints, Tab demanded.

Bossy ;) Can't say I mind a bit of ordering about x

Hence reserves and your hot sarge?

Oooh yeah :D Not sure about the uniform though :S It's a bit too baggy ;) 2 much left to the imagination!!

Like it a bit blatant then? ;) Tab dared, and felt his heart beginning to pick up. What was he doing? They'd—okay, *he'd*—not flirted this much before. This was outright flirting, too. This was almost…well. He shifted uncomfortably. It *was* sexy.

Sometimes :P Subtle has its place, but some dirty talk is defs where its at ;) Specially in the form of orders.

No questions asked?

Neverrrr x

OK, Tab replied. *List your top five kinks. Now.*

Instantly, a *;)* was returned, and then there was a short pause. Just as Tab had decided Demi had been put off, his email notification was set off, and he opened the newcomer from *Demi J. [Maxi's bro]* with a weird mixture of trepidation and excitement that made his stomach clench.

1) Being given such a blatant order ;) You're goooood, tabby-cat!!

2) Sense dep. Like can't see, can't touch, whatevs. Makes u FOCUS. Sexy as hell.

3) 1 of u having your kit still on. Prefs me but not fussy ;) Can't beat keeping someone at ur mercy for a bit (ok ok I can't explain this one it's just dead on)

(Tab laughed at the third one…)

4) Guys mouth, my collarbone—S'ALL I'M SAYING.

(…and made a mental note of the fourth, because that sounded weirdly interesting.)

5) There is no fifth one, what do u think I am, a porn star?????

Tab sniggered, and returned to his texts, tapping out a new one slowly as he turned over the list in his head. Finally, he decided on the first one. *That wasn't five,* he scolded. *You'll have to be punished if u disobey orders.*

5—getting a good punishing, then ;) New one! came the exuberant reply. *What about u, tabby-cat? Bet u like a good stroking ;) and cats always get themselves in positions they can't get out of!!*

Tab choked, laughed, and choked again, startled. Demi was right—subtle was not his thing. Or Tab's, judging by the very physical response the text generated. He groaned, and threw a book across his bedroom. It bounced off the edge of the door, and slammed it shut.

Never got myself in a position I couldn't get out of, he retorted.

Bendy, are u? ;)

FLIRT.

U seem kind of stuck now, fancy a hand???

Tab flushed hotly, and eyed the door. Once he was sure it had closed properly, and Aunt JuliKate hadn't yelled at him for slamming it, he popped the button on his jeans and eased down the zip.

Got 2 of my own ;) he replied.

Fancy 1 more anyway??? Demi asked instantly. *I've had loads of practise @ stroking things :D*

Tab bit his lip, one hand idly lingering around the waistband of his briefs. It really shouldn't be so hot. It *really* shouldn't. He'd never even *met* Demi.

I've had plenty enough @ stroking this thing, Tab replied eventually.

Not others? U need to expand ur horizons! x

1 other. And expand to where???

Every1 has something to play with ;) came the (wise?) reply. Dickish reply, definitely, and Tab wondered vaguely if Demi were just toying with him, or if Demi were in a similar state. If Demi was…enjoying flirting with him, and turning him on, or if Demi even realised he'd done it.

Part of Tab—the part of his brain that (supposedly) commanded his dick—hoped Demi *was* in the same state.

U could always play w/ mine ;) Demi said eventually, and Tab didn't have the blood to flush anymore. He pushed his fingers under the cotton. *Share and share alike, im generous ;)*

Slut.

Totes! xxx

U probably have things.

I got plenty of things ;) but nothing bad. All sunshine and daisies, me. Fucking in the sunshine and daisies, anyway x

Ur impossible.

Im a sexy-ass dweeb and u no u want this. u were the one giving the orders anyway, so its ur fault!!

Im ordering u to shut up and put ur hand down ur pants.

Waaaay ahead of u sir xxx

Tab groaned aloud, muting it with the back of the phone when it came out *too* loud, at the confirmation. He wasn't the only one. Demi was…Demi was doing it, too, so he'd done it on purpose, so…

He couldn't muster the brainpower to think, and dropped the phone for later. His brain drifted for a moment, trying to find something to latch onto, to *focus* on, to draw on.

It imagined Nick crouched over him, that deep raspy voice murmuring, "You seem kind of stuck now." He'd do things before suggesting them. One of those intense, powerful hands would fit over Tab's, so that technically he *only* touched Tab's hand, but the *intent* would be clear in those blue eyes. "Fancy a hand?" he'd say.

Tab came apart on his own, to Demi's words and Nick's image, and had never felt so *torn*.

Chapter 14

THE INTERCLUB WAS on the Saturday after that. Tab had been looking forward to it for weeks, mostly to get to watch Nick in action proper, but after Nick and Demi had just *merged* like that in his head...

Uncle Eddie had hired a minibus, because the other club was two towns over, and Tab had tried to beg off after helping him load up the kit, but no dice. Eddie had just snorted and clapped him on the shoulder (and nearly taken his *arm* off, holy shit) and said, "Not passing up a chance to talk to your Nick, are you?"

"He's not my Nick," Tab mumbled, flushing hotly.

"Not until you tell him," Eddie said agreeably, and shook his head. "Nope, you're coming. Kate's having the girls round and wants us both out for the day. And you know how she gets!"

Tab did know. But it didn't help.

"We'll miss visiting Mum," he tried feebly.

"We'll go tomorrow."

Tab regretted letting Uncle Eddie work out he liked Nick. Uncle Eddie got so *stupid* sometimes, but he wasn't being swayed, and Tab grudgingly lurked on the minibus as the students began to arrive. And his mood really, *really* wasn't helped when Nick—

fucking gorgeous *arse*—rocked up on a *motorbike* and in heavy *leathers* and *argh!*

Tab, quite frankly, would have quite appreciated being smited by a vengeful God at that moment. Any God at all; the faith wasn't the important thing. Anything but the sinister leer of any of the Lust Gods, to be quite frank.

"Alright, mate?"

The seat beside him thunked, and Tab's higher functions all—simultaneously—committed suicide. "Errrr," he gurgled.

"Coming to watch us kick arse, or are you the honorary nurse?" Nick asked, and grinned. Tab's gut melted and pooled...well, lower down. Which he didn't need. Just the *thought* of Nick the other day...

He felt very fucking betrayed by his own body, and crossed his legs under his bag. Thank God for no-space-minibuses and having to keep your bag on your lap.

"Aunt JuliKate's having one of those days," he croaked eventually.

"Unlucky," Nick said, casually raising a hand to high-five one of the other boys as he scrambled aboard, but never taking his eyes off Tab. "You, uh, actually coming to the fight or you just hitching a ride and sodding off later?"

Tab shrugged. "Dunno."

"'Cause, uh..." Nick shrugged, lifting a hand to rub the back of his neck. He pinked faintly, and Tab stared in fascination, the semi in his jeans suddenly forgotten. "I need a word with you later."

Oh.

Oh.

Ohhhh holy-fucknutting-Madonna-on-a-stick. Shit. Shit shit shit *shiiiit.* Nick was like telepathic or something, right? He totally had to be. He *knew*—somehow he *knew* that Tab had...had...

"And for the record, breathing is cool," Nick said casually, the pink colour receding. Could you transmit a blush? Because Nick was totally transmitting a blush—as he paled, Tab felt his own face heat up. Stupid. Fucking. Body.

"Oh shut up," Tab mumbled, and blew upwards into his fringe. "I'm nearly done with those comics your baby sister wants."

"Cool," Nick said, and so dismissively that Tab frowned. "I'm guessing you've not seen the fight list?"

"Uh, no." Why would he care? Nick was like scary good, whoever he was going to spar with he'd destroy, no problem.

"You should've," Nick said, and a slow grin spread from left to right across Nick's face. "I got Allen."

"Who?"

"Allen. As in, the f-word?"

Tab blinked. Allen. Allen who had called him a faggot, who Nick had gotten in trouble for hitting, who…inadvertently, had given Tab that horrible ray of hope and the *choice* between Nick and Demi.

"Kill him."

Nick laughed.

"Seriously," Tab said. "Kill him. Like. I don't know the rules or anything—"

"You *live* in a boxing gym and you don't know the *rules?*"

"—but if you—shut up—don't absolutely destroy him and smash him into little bits of pulp and put the pulp in a matchbox and post the pulp home to his mother—then I'm telling my uncle *you* called me the f-word, and you'll get kicked out of the gym, too," Tab finished breathlessly.

If not for Allen, he would be happily imagining Nick to be *entirely* impossible and horrified by gay people, and he could have blissfully gone off with Demi by now. Jerk. So Allen needed to die. *Now.*

"Wo-ow," Nick said slowly, then smirked and leaned forward so his face was less than an inch from Tab's. Kissing distance. Dear God. Tab swallowed, and felt his blood sinking along with the movement. "And just a hint? Don't threaten me again."

Nick's voice was very low, very raspy, and very fucking hot. Tab swallowed again, and clutched his bag a little tighter.

"But," Nick continued, "I guess I could fuck up his face a bit."

He leaned back, and twisted to respond to something one of the other boys yelled from the back, but Tab didn't hear it over the sound of his own heartbeat in his ears.

And it was saying *'you're-fucked, you're-fucked, you're-fucked.'*

THE OTHER GYM was bigger than Uncle Eddie's, but Tab vaguely remembered it as being less busy. They had an annual interclub, and Eddie's exuberant, "Bob! How's the brats!" trumpeted from the minivan window said that *this* interclub hadn't fallen on Aunt JuliKate's girls' day by coincidence.

Bob Tucker, one of Eddie's own students from years back, was waiting in the gym car park, surrounded by his own students. Most of them grinned or nodded at the bus, but Tab's eyes were drawn straight to Allen in the midst of them.

"How'd he get into another gym anyway?" he whispered to Nick, who snorted.

"Loads of gyms ignore the licensing rules," he said, and shrugged. "And to be fair, he was just a twat and there's loads of professional boxers who're twats anyway."

Tab scowled. Allen, eyeing him right back across the yard, scowled back.

"Kill him anyway," he said, and Nick snorted, grinning.

"You're savage, mate. Got your claws out today and everything."

"Tab, c'mon, let's help Bob get the ring set up," Uncle Eddie called.

Tab started forward, and Nick's arm shot out to catch him under the elbow. "I need to talk to you after the fight," he said, and the smile was gone. Those stern eyebrows were turned down, and the mouth a grim slash. And quite frankly, Tab ought to try atheism, because whatever version of Cupid his one-man religion had *sucked*. Even Nick's scary motherfucker face was hot.

"Tab! Inside!" Uncle Eddie yelled, and disappeared through the glass doors with Bob. Most of the other students—of both gyms—filtered in after them, but Allen unstuck his feet from the floor and approached, even as Tab pulled his arm free and awkwardly nodded.

"You heard him," Allen said lowly. "Inside. *Tab.*" His eyes, however, were fixed on Nick.

"Sorry, did I say something that sounded like 'hi, Allen, how's your day?'" Nick demanded, cutting off any reply Tab might have made. "We were having a chat here, now fuck off."

"Just so you know," Allen said quietly, "I don't give a fuck about your little gay thing you two are up to—"

Tab flamed red. Nick rolled his eyes.

"—but I don't lose to queers."

"Oh *honey,*" Nick said, his voice suddenly rising an octave and developing an odd nasal slur. "If you wanted a gay thing, all you had to do was ask."

Allen's face twisted.

"Nick…" Tab said warningly, glancing towards the doors. There was no alarm button out here, and if they started brawling then Uncle Eddie would go mental and then Nick wouldn't get to murder the jerk in the ring *properly.*

"Listen," Nick snarled, voice dropping back to normal. He stepped forward and squared off in one smooth motion, that steely face suddenly cold. "I get it. You're a prick. That's cool. But I am a much better boxer than you, and to top it off, I don't like you. If you leave that ring with your nose still attached to your fucking *face,* count yourself lucky."

"You threatening me?"

"Promising," Nick growled. His voice came from his gut, and Tab shivered, curling his toes in his shoes. Which was *totally* inappropriate right now.

"Don't promise what you can't deliver," Allen hissed lowly.

"Oh I can deliver," Nick said sharply. "Especially when you won't fucking touch me, tosser. Too scared to get the gay on your gloves."

Allen ground his teeth audibly, and Tab pulled on Nick's elbow. "Leave it," he said. "Kill him in the ring, don't start here."

"Why don't you listen to your *boyfriend?*"

"And kill you later? Sure," Nick said, and smiled. It was a shark smile. It was completely ice-cold, and Tab fisted his other hand in his jacket pocket. Why. The hell. Was he finding Nick-the-dangerous-fucknut so *hot?* He needed therapy, seriously.

"Just so you know," Allen called as Nick turned away towards the doors, and Tab closed his eyes, groaning. Great. Just great. "I could destroy you."

"How's that?"

Allen shrugged. "Bet your boxing buddies wouldn't be pleased to hear about the queer in their midst."

Nick stopped.

"Nick."

Tab wanted to drag him into the gym by the arm. And knew he couldn't. And…simultaneously…kind of didn't want to either.

Nick turned back to Allen and slowly approached until Allen backed up. Tab didn't miss the flash of fear, and maybe Tab was a prick, too, because *dear God*, that felt good to see. And Nick just…just didn't stop. He didn't stop until Allen was backed against the minibus, and Nick was less than an inch away.

And oh God, Allen *had* to be a fucked-up freak because how he could not just…just launch and snog Nick's face off at that distance was completely beyond Tab. *He* would. Oh God, he wouldn't have even thought twice about it.

"Bad move," Nick hissed, so low that Tab found himself inching forward to hear properly. "Because guess what, fuckface? Everybody. Knows. Everybody knows which team I'm batting for. But I'm willing to bet nobody knows *yours.*"

Allen paled—and so did Tab.

Everybody knew—what? That Nick was…

No. No *way*. No—fucking—*way*. It was completely impossible. Completely and utterly fucking impossible. Not—no way.

"Like I said," Nick breathed into the stunned silence, "if you leave that ring with your nose attached to your face, you should count yourself lucky."

This time when Nick turned away, Tab didn't notice his face or his aggression or—anything. He felt too tight-chested. There was a roaring in his ears and his gods—all of them, every last one—had deserted him. Nick couldn't be…he just meant in *general*, right? He meant that nobody would believe Allen if he said Nick was gay. That's what he meant. It *had* to be.

"Tab!" Uncle Eddie's voice boomed, and his figure appeared in the doorway. "When I said come and help set up, I meant now!"

Nick edged around him and disappeared into the gym; Allen

slowly inched away from the minibus, scowl fixed in place, and Tab replied to his uncle's questioning expression by simply shaking his head and sending up a quick and silent prayer to the Supreme God.

Don't let this be happening, he begged. He was already being torn in two—please, God, don't muddy the waters further by letting Nick be…

He fumbled for his phone as he slipped into the gym and crossed the lobby. He texted Demi. *Crisis,* he said. *I think the boxer just admitted to being gay.*

When, not twenty seconds later, Demi asked, *Y is that a crisis???* Tab switched his phone off entirely and took a deep, cleansing breath.

He was completely, utterly, one hundred percent *fucked*—and all because apparently waiting your whole life for a hot available gay guy to come along made the God of fucking Luck think it would be *funny* to send you two.

"Fuck my life," he told the changing room doors.

It seemed like the only appropriate thing to say.

Chapter 15

BY THE TIME Nick's fight came around, Tab had…composed himself. Ish.

He had armed himself with his notebook and a pencil, and maybe it wasn't the best way to handle things and maybe it would get him funny looks from everyone, but *fuck it*. He was going to do what he always did at times of crisis—draw. Portraits took time and effort to be good; portraits took concentration and realism and skill.

Maybe comics did for other people, too, but not Tab. Tab could whack out a rough comic sketch in five minutes, and now…well. Now he'd do it in three. Peanuts, after all, didn't take long to draw at all.

And by the time Nick's fight came around, Tab had gotten a bit of practice in. You know. To calm himself down and—not think about what Nick had said to Allen out there.

It wasn't easy, though, when Nick ducked through the ropes looking so…focused. Uncle Eddie was checking his gloves, and Nick was just *staring* at Allen from under his eyebrows. And he might be…he could be.

Tab touched pencil to paper, and waited.

Because if he was gay…if Nick were gay, then—maybe Tab

could have him? But if he did…if he did, he couldn't have Demi—and vice versa, really. There was no way to have both and Nick was gorgeous and all, but Demi had gotten under Tab's skin somewhere along the line and…

U no u want this.

He did. But he wanted Nick, too. And…

"I want a *fair* fight," Uncle Eddie said seriously, and someone sniggered. Allen bared his—mouth-guard?—and Nick smirked. "Seriously, boys."

Tab silently hoped Nick was being telepathic again, and thought *smash his face in* as loudly as he could.

The sound of the bell rippled through the room, and—Nick didn't move.

Tab had sneakily watched the odd sparring session through the glass doors at Grangefields, and had seen Nick at the bags enough to know that he moved when he boxed. He bounced on his toes, he darted, he shifted around. He was almost restless, and yet…

When the gong sounded, he simply hunched in on himself, shoulders up and gloves raised in front of his face. It was like a snake coiling tighter, and Tab's pencil froze, immobile, on the paper. *Move!* he called in his head. *Kill him! Move!*

Allen had no such problems—he darted forward, lashing out in rapid, twisting strikes. They were stupid fast, like gunfire, the sound of leather on skin (and when Nick parried, leather on leather) loud and harsh in the quiet, cavernous room. He kept his distance—nipping in and slipping away again in an instant—and struck with the arm fully extended, reaching out instead of closing in. A dancer's way of boxing. The coward's way, Uncle Eddie had always called it. The way of someone not big enough or heavy enough or *tough* enough to take a good solid blow.

And yet Nick didn't bother to retaliate, batting his blows aside and finally moving only to coax Allen into an almost circling motion.

Kill him, Tab thought loudly. *Knock his teeth out. Give him a black eye. Do it. Do it!*

And like magic, as if Nick had heard him—

He closed in and exploded. It was like a burst of motion; the heavy *bumph-bup, bumph-bup* leather on skin now, not leather on leather. There was no way Tab could capture this in portrait: the sheer speed, the brutal focus in Nick's eyes, the tense-snap-release shift of his muscles. He didn't box; he *danced*. He was all grace and instinct; he was breathtakingly dangerous, deadly beautiful, and Tab felt both a yearning in his chest, and an ache in his stomach.

Nick was downright stunning.

And yet Demi…

He would have to stop the flirts with Demi. He would have to stop texting him, stop the funny, nerdy little chats and the steadily increasing dirty talk. He would have to give him up, and yet—

U no u want this.

They circled each other, breaking apart for a moment as though gathering strength, and then in one fluid motion they crashed together in a violent grapple, a snarl twisting Nick's features, pure aggression wrought into Allen's, and Tab could find his own heart picking up in response, some primal *want* curling around his fingers. The pencil was shaking. He wanted to move, wanted to stand up and shout with the other boys, wanted to burst out of his stillness and *do something*…

And he saw it. The moment that Allen dropped his left arm just a little too far, the moment that he turned a little too wide…and the way Nick's eyes narrowed like a sniper finding the target. The way that Nick's right arm punched outwards from his shoulder and chest, ramrod straight and every muscle highlighted under the pale skin. The way the skin rippled as the glove made contact; the way, when it did, that Allen's jaw was forced so loose from the rest of his face.

Tab saw it all, like slow-motion, and then Allen's mouth-guard skittered across the floor of the ring and he dropped. His body hit the boards with a rattling *th'dunk* and Nick stepped back, returning to the coiled, *waiting* stillness from before.

Allen spat onto the floor of the ring, pushed himself up on one elbow—and fell back down. He looked wide-eyed and startled—and the entire room knew concussion when they saw it. Bob Tucker was shouting for quiet and some 'bloody fucking decorum, boys!' even as the noise level exploded, and Nick fell back to the ropes, dropping his hands and rolling his shoulders. When Eddie held out the dish, he spat his mouth-guard out into the water and grinned around those crooked, smashed teeth.

"You fancy telling the lads our little secret, Allen?" he taunted loudly.

"Nick…" Uncle Eddie said warningly.

"Allen," Nick continued loudly, and Tab felt his stomach somehow—impossibly—soar and drop at the same time, "apparently didn't want to get beaten by a *queer.*"

And then Nick's meaning became clear, when every guy from Grangefields snorted as one. The wave of derisive disbelief was crystal-clear, and it was like the clouds parting after rain. *That* was what Nick had meant. He was so straight that *everyone* knew. Nobody would *believe* Allen.

And it meant that he was impossible. It meant that Tab's choice was made for him. It meant that Nick was *safe*, and that he could try and shrug this off, and turn to Demi, and erase the image of Nick, naked in bed, and murmuring Demi's words. Tab didn't have to fucking *choose.*

The euphoria that burst like a firework in his chest was nothing to do with Nick's victory.

Tab dropped his notebook when he jumped up, and the pencil skittered across the floor. Nick's chest was heaving, his skin was gleaming, and the look in his eye was a vicious kind of pleasure. He was beautiful and he was straight and Tab could finally just *get on with it* now.

Nick dropped down into the melee of other fighters, almost welcomed home by them, grinning at his reception and dark-eyed and dizzy in the way that Tab had seen a thousand newly-graded students by now, and when he broke free, Tab met him there on the mats.

And for a moment, complete madness overtook Tab's mind. For a moment, all he could see was that mouth, that crooked set of lips in the midst of such a harsh and perfect face, and his brain wondered—just for a moment—what they would feel like. If they would be soft, or as harsh as the sharp cheekbones that framed the danger in his face.

For a split second, he moved to kiss Nick—

And then the rest of his brain kicked in. *Red alert!* Do *not* kiss the guy who just beat someone up for calling him gay, then mocked him for it in front of fifty people! *Back up! Back up!*

Only it was too late to back up. He had a hand on Nick's shoulder; Nick's face was right there, inches from Tab's, and there was some unidentifiable god or demon lurking around them like a shadow just *screaming* for Tab to…

He changed the motion, clumsily, and hugged Nick instead.

"Uh," he mumbled. "Well done. Um. Yeah."

Tab let go with a faint sucking noise, the sweat on Nick's bare torso clinging to his clothes. *Gross.*

"Uh," Nick echoed, hands still held out and encased in the heavy gloves. "Thanks?"

"Um," Tab said, then ducked away. "You go get…changed and stuff. You reek."

"Thanks?" Nick repeated in a bemused tone, then the very tip of a tongue darted out to touch his lips. "We need to talk later."

"Yeah," Tab lied. "Sure."

The moment Nick was gone, Tab gathered up his pencil and notebook and retreated to the minibus. He was going to text Demi, and start forgetting about definitely-straight Nick, and make a decision already.

And the notebook was blank. He hadn't drawn a thing.

After that…

After that, Tab didn't see Nick for two whole weeks. He avoided the boxer for the rest of the day, and sat up front with Uncle Eddie on the drive home, and ducked into the flat the minute they got back to Grangefields. He swapped his shifts around at the gym to avoid Nick's times. He *avoided* Nick, and it was the only way to shake off his crush. Ever gone up against a Crush

God? It's not an easy fight to win.

But Tab was determined to win it. Because Nick was straight, and Demi was gay, and…and that was that. That was his choice, right there. And he had to get his head out of Nick-space and into Demi-space.

Which wasn't easy. Even spending most of those two weeks at college, burying himself in the nearly-finished portrait didn't quite let him forget about…

About the fight. About the near-kiss. About wanking to Demi's words and Nick's voice. Putting it bluntly.

He focused instead on the portrait, using the pictures to finish it. Watercolour streaked the red gloves into a violent motion; smudged wax creating the battered-but-strong punchbag. The darkness of the charcoal background brought out Nick's pale tones, and the mixtures of tan and pink and pure white streaked a spotlight across the boxer's focused face.

Tab was especially proud of the eyes. That exact shade of brown-green-gold had been impossible, so he'd ground fir leaves into a mulch and used that, covering it in clear nail polish for the sheen and preservation.

But.

(There was always a but.)

But it wasn't Nick. Not quite. There was always something missing—and that something hurt. It wasn't just missing from the portrait, it was missing from those two weeks, too. Demi was quieter—or maybe it was Tab—but the texts weren't enough, and the flirty edge wasn't there anymore. He tried to think about Demi, but found that curly hair falling away and the perfect smile twisting and reshaping itself.

I think, was Demi's horrible advice when Tab turned to him, *that if ur this wound up bcos ur avoiding ur boxer then u need 2 talk 2 him.*

I can't, Tab had replied that time. *He's straight. There's no point. I need to forget about him.*

Did u ask him?

Does it matter?

DID U ASK HIM

No! Tab admitted. *But i didn't have 2 ok? he made it obvious.*

Demi hadn't replied to that. He'd stopped replying a lot lately. He'd push Tab to talk to Nick, then go quiet. The flirting had died off, and Tab missed that, too. He'd even started dreaming about it—much to his horror—when the little messages that had been so fun and so sneaky and so heartwarming just…twisted up on themselves and became whispers, in a low, harsh voice.

Im not sure u made the right choice tabby-cat, Demi said, two weeks after the interclub. *Talk 2 him.*

When Tab woke in the middle of that night from a weird Nick-Demi-threeway dream, he knew that Nick being straight hadn't solved a fucking *thing*.

Chapter 16

ON SATURDAY, TAB went to see Mum by himself.

He didn't usually anymore. It was too hard, the pain of losing her without quite losing her too sharp. But every now and then he figured he should make the effort, because she'd been Mum for years, and maybe she wasn't *Mum*-Mum anymore, but she was still...you know. Mum.

It made sense. It did.

Jon wasn't there when he arrived, Eddie dropping him off at the hospital entrance with a paternal look and a squeeze of the shoulder, but Nurse Aggie was, and she took him into the locked ward this time. It was always quiet in the locked ward—the result of drugs to keep everyone calm—but Mum's little room was a beacon of warm light, and Toby Gibson, one of the mental health team that overlooked Mum's care, was sitting in the visitor's chair.

"Hello, Tab," he smiled genially.

"Hi," Tab said.

The room had changed from last time. He didn't usually come here—*usually*, if Mum was okay to have visitors, they took her out into the main unit. But sometimes she was kind of...between. And now was one of those times, because the walls were covered in huge sheets of paper and she was painting with her bare hands and talking to herself—singing, muttering, chattering, warbling—and. . .

Tab nodded. Aggie left them to it. "Hi, Mum," Tab said.

Mum had been pretty once, but hospital had paled all the freckles away, and washed the gold hair to a simpler blonde. They cut it for her, too. She'd always had very long hair, but the hospital cut it. They didn't make her wear shoes—she hadn't worn shoes since Tab was *tiny*—and she floated around in her too-big nightie. She was skinny now, which was weird. Tab remembered hugs like being smothered in a sofa, all burning joss sticks and candles. Now she didn't hug, and she smelled like hospital.

"I've got an exhibition coming up at the college," he said. "Are you going to come?"

"Ssh," Mum murmured, a blue starfish handprint embossing itself onto the last blank sheet. None of the papers were *of* anything, that Tab could tell. "Ssh. You'll disturb the flow. The rhythm. Everything in rhythm."

Tab swallowed.

"Everything has rhythm," Mum whispered. "Voice, song. Music. The music is lovely." She began to hum.

"Aunt—Uncle—Uncle Julian's nearly done with, um, the treatment," Tab said. Sometimes she knew who Kate was, and sometimes she got upset and cried about missing things. She'd never met *Kate*, not really. "Um, you know. Becoming Kate. She's started going out with Eddie to pubs and stuff now."

"*Ssh,*" Mum insisted. "You'll *disturb* things. Everything has to be *perfect*."

Tab sighed, a little shakily. He felt oddly bruised this time. Sometimes he came and talked and went and it was okay, it was fine. He was used to Mum being loopy and painting on the walls. She'd done that even before the hospital. But with the portrait and Nick and Demi and everything that had been just silly fun getting somehow weirdly serious, and Demi flirting and Nick not being as impenetrable and impossible as Tab had supposed, and then *being* impossible again and the crush still not going away. . .

He felt. . .oddly. . .fragile.

He folded his arms over his chest and hunched his shoulders. "There's this boy," he said eventually.

Mum paused. "A boy."

"Yeah," Tab said, pushing the moment of—of attention, maybe not quite lucidity. "Two boys, actually. One's funny and sweet, and the other's gorgeous and sticks up for me, but I can't have both."

Mum smiled, wide and beatific, like a flower blooming at speed. "Of course you can," she murmured. "Don't limit yourself. Have everything. Have the world. As long as it's in rhythm. Where's Edward?"

Tab paused. "Uncle Eddie?" His name was Edmund, not Edward.

"Edward," Mum insisted. "I've told him. Dad's told him. He's not to use that silly nickname."

"Oh-kay," Tab said slowly. Edward *was* Granddad, not Uncle Eddie.

Toby, over Tab's shoulder, sighed and pushed his glasses up his nose. "She seems to be developing some confusion with time," he said quietly.

"Don't talk about me like I'm not *here*!" Mum exploded, sounding suddenly childish, and kicked a pot of paint against the wall. Tab backed out of the room, practised at knowing when there'd be a response, and Aggie pushed past him into it, already chiding.

"*Serenity*, what'd you go and do that for!" she scolded, and Mum kicked another.

Toby withdrew as well, the sympathetic look in place until they walked back out to the main ward, and then it gave way to his professional face. "Like I said," he sighed, "she's developing some confusion with time. Not too dissimilar to a dementia patient."

Tab liked Tony. Tony told him stuff. Tony didn't act like Tab was a kid. All the other doctors and nurses did, acted like Tab was too young to know this stuff, and fuck that. He'd been looking after Mum since forever. He had to know these things, too. And Tony *got* that.

"It looks like it's coming and going with her episodes," Tony continued, readjusting his glasses again. "It's early days yet, we're still working on that part."

"How's Josie?" Tab asked bitterly.

"Oh, much better," Tony said, and smiled. "She's turning up less frequently the past couple of weeks, so there *is* progress."

From the locked ward, there was a bang and a shriek, and Tony sighed, turning back towards the doors.

"I won't be a minute," he promised, and vanished, but Tab didn't want to give him a minute. He backed out of the ward entirely, feeling a heat behind his eyes, poking and burning. He hovered in the main corridor for a minute, torn between staying and going, and then going won out. She was obviously on an edge. Something was going on again. She didn't realise Uncle Eddie hadn't come, and she wouldn't...she wouldn't know he'd gone.

So he went, stalking back out into the normal bits of the hospital, and if the corridors were blurry, so what? Mum was in the ward, she'd be...safe. Okay. It was better than leaving her on her own, where she could hurt herself or somebody else or just do something silly, something her fits and voices let her forget, like switching the gas off or eating or...

He wiped the back of his hand furiously over his eyes. It was better. It *was*.

"Hey!" a deep voice called. "Oi! Tab!"

His trainers squealed on the tiles as he stopped dead and blinked back angry tears, trying to squash the hurt and impotent fury and recall the voice that had called him. He turned, and there in the doorway of a ward—eight, though Tab didn't know what kind of people were in ward eight—stood, of all people, Nick.

Tab's stomach wrenched painfully, torn between horror at Nick seeing him like this, at Nick maybe working out when he'd said Mum was gone he actually meant gone-here, not gone-dead, and...and just not caring what Nick thought, for the first time ever, because she'd been *Mum*.

Nick padded from the door to stand in front of him, frowning. He was in baggy jeans and a black hoodie, the red logo of Uncle Eddie's gym across the front. He'd shaved his head again, the hair almost totally gone, and he looked tired. There were lines around his eyes. He was wound up himself—but then, Tab supposed nobody looked happy in a hospital.

"I'd ask if you were okay, but..." Nick eyed him, and shrugged.

"Yeah. Well."

"You've been avoiding me."

Something twinged, and Tab ignored it. "Just been busy," he lied.

"Uh-huh," Nick said, and frowned, eyes scanning Tab's face. A slow flush crept up Tab's neck, and he swallowed hard, breaking eye contact to stare at the floor and wish—bitterly—that he could just...just hug him, or...

Or forget he existed and be able to go for Demi. Forget that there would always be that question mark over it if he did.

"What's up?"

Nick's voice was suddenly very low, very soft—albeit still with that underlying rasp, like damp sandpaper—and Tab's lip wobbled involuntarily. And dangerously.

"Been visiting my mum," he managed, and hated the way his voice sounded. Thin and reedy. Close to cracking.

"Your—" Nick started, then glanced over his shoulder at the sign for the mental health unit. "Oh."

"Yeah," Tab croaked.

"Bad day, then?"

Tab bit down hard on his lip, hard enough to taste metal, and Nick groaned, a deep and reverberating kind of sound.

"C'mere," he mumbled, and then a warm hand was on the back of Tab's neck and his face in rough cotton and he could smell some cheap, standard deodorant, and the edges of leather, and feel a molten heat flooding off Nick's shoulder and chest, and a rock-hard body under too-loose clothes.

He clung back, the stupid misery shaken up a little by the shock offering, and clutched fistfuls of the black fabric.

Nick's hands were around his back. He was fractionally taller than Tab, which Tab hadn't noticed before, and he stood solid as a tree, but he hugged warm and hard and...and like Tab kind of needed. Like he wanted Nick to hug.

"Sorry," he mumbled.

"S'fine."

Tab sniffed, pressing his forehead into the top of Nick's shoulder and breathing in deeply through his mouth before crushing the hurt and trying to give the mortification a bit of breathing room. Because Nick was hugging him, and he had to look a sight, and...and...

He let go. Nick's hands lingered on his elbows for a minute before dropping and those still surprisingly smooth hands vanished into the hoodie pocket. "What're you doing here?" Tab mumbled, scrubbing the edge of his sleeve under his eyes.

"Visiting," Nick said. "Bored now though." He rolled his eyes, the lines easing momentarily, and Tab cracked a watery smile. "Grandma's come down. It's a nightmare."

"I'm sorry," Tab breathed.

"Nah, she fractured her wrist," Nick said and waved a hand flippantly. "But she's putting on the full 'I'm old and frail and won't be here forever' so the whole family's flocked in, and she's *that* type of grandma."

"What type?"

Nick pointed at a red mark on his cheek.

"Oh," Tab said, and sniffed again. "Lucky you. My Nana's a grumpy old bat."

"Want to escape for a bit?" Nick suggested, still in that slightly-low, slightly-soft tone. "I know the staff at the pub round the corner."

"Your grandma'll miss you."

"My grandma has like fifteen grandkids, with two cheeks each. That's like forty pinches."

"Thirty."

"Whatever. Still take her a while to get back to me," Nick said dismissively, and Tab managed a shaky little laugh. "C'mon. My round."

"M'only seventeen."

"Just as well I'm eighteen, then, innit?" Nick said, pulling Tab around by the shoulder. "Lucky you're here, I was about to go a bit mental myself. She's only sixty-two, but she's carrying on like she's ninety. She still does that Race for Life guff, for Christ's sake."

"Hypochondriac?" Tab suggested, the burning beginning to recede from his face. Maybe...maybe if he could get over Nick, then Nick could…could be a friend.

"A what now?"

"A hypochondriac. You know, those people who sneeze and immediately think they have lung cancer."

Nick laughed. "Yeah, that's her."

They fell into step as they passed out of the hospital doors, and Nick's hand dropped from Tab's shoulder. Tab kind of…didn't want it to.

"It's just hard sometimes," he blurted out. "'Cause she's not Mum anymore, not really, but she looks like Mum. And it hurts sometimes."

Nick hummed, hands in pockets again. It was raining lightly outside, barely more than a mist.

"I know it's really girly and shit, but I love my mum and it hurts."

"S'not girly and shit," Nick said. "Everyone should love their mum. Unless your mum's, like, crazy violent or locks you in cellars and stuff."

Tab smiled, something soothing by the matter-of-fact tone and the…the easy understanding. Even if Nick didn't understand, because of course he didn't, but…he didn't judge either.

"Dumbest thing to do in your uncle's gym, right, it's insult someone's mum," Nick continued. "Sisters aren't smart either. But fucking hell. I once sounded off at Gary Noah—y'know, that dark kid in advanced now with the hellish good right hook—about his mum, next thing I know, I'm in A&E and *my* mum is calling me all sorts. Was a fucking good shot though, I have to hand it to him."

Tab grinned a little. He did remember that, he thought. It was just about when he'd joined the gym. He was pretty sure he remembered anyway, because Uncle Eddie had told him to call an ambulance for someone who'd been knocked out, and then two days later *Nick* had turned up with two black eyes and a broken nose, and…

Tab opened his mouth, ready to finally say something, and the moment he thought seriously about it, The Fear took over and he shut his trap again. *Don't ruin this,* he scolded himself. *He's being nice, don't ruin it by saying you fancy him. He might even be nice about it, but he'll reject you anyway. He's straight. He said so. He's got Luce.*

"Why'd you come out to see me?" he mumbled.

"Coincidence," Nick said, holding the door to the pub. It was a quiet street-corner type; the barman looked even younger than Tab, high-fived Nick wordlessly, and nodded at the Fosters pump. "Yeah, go on, Rob. Cheers. Nah, coincidence," Nick repeated. "Was going to the canteen actually. Hospital air makes me thirsty."

"Alcoholic."

"Working on it," Nick grinned. Tab's heart skipped a beat. Maybe two. Three. Okay, whatever, it went for a full-on attack. "Actually, I was gonna tell you something next time I saw you, tried to at the interclub, but fuck it. Not the time now."

"Next time?"

"Yeah, next time. If you don't run away again. Cheers," Nick handed him a pint, and clanked the glasses. "So what's wrong with your mum?"

"She hears voices. She has this, like, imaginary friend. And she has bad days, when she attacks people and stuff," Tab shrugged awkwardly. "She went into hospital a couple of years ago and I had to live with Nana and then Uncle Eddie. She…she tried to hurt me with some nail scissors."

"Shit," Nick said, almost conversationally, as they sat at a table in the corner. Apart from two old geezers doing a crossword and arguing how to spell 'verb', they were the only customers there.

"She was always a bit loopy, but she got worse, and then…yeah. They sectioned her and I went to live with Uncle Eddie."

"Still. Job and college and shit. You're not doing too bad."
Tab hummed.

"You're like…clever. And good. Those comics you do are epic, you know. Portrait's not too bad."

"Please," Tab snorted.

"Think you overdid the makin' me look good thing, but hey, your show."

Tab rolled his eyes. "You're not ugly."

Nick snorted. "I don't even have half my real teeth. Six fakes."

"What happened?"

Nick shrugged. "Some kid," he said flatly.

"When…when you were bullied?"

"…Last time. Yeah. Made me sort myself out," Nick said, and

grinned crookedly again. Fake or not, the broken smile was still stupidly sexy. "Still dumb, though."

"You're not stupid either," Tab said. He thought about kicking Nick under the table, but decided not to risk it.

"Oh trust me, I am," Nick said, smirking over the top of his pint, then he set it down and leaned forward. "Don't even know what hyper-condy-mack means."

"Hypochondriac."

"That too."

Tab half-smiled and shook his head. Since when was stupid hot?

"Don't let your mum and that get to you, 'kay? You and your peanuts, you're gonna get somewhere special. Kid like you ain't sticking to a nowhere like this forever."

Tab bit his lip. "And you'll go to South America."

"Maybe one day. But that's just money. You—that's something else. You got something cool going on there."

Tab opened his mouth again, wanting to say that he didn't, and he was just scribbling and waiting for his life to become something that wasn't just the gym and a crazy mother and that constant ache in his gut now because even though now he knew he couldn't have Nick and he could have Demi, he was still going to lose. He would always be wondering if Nick would have been better, always looking for someone more like him, and how was that fair on Demi? He was always going to *lose*.

And then he didn't say anything, because…because who was Tab kidding? He was just this dorky kid who drew comics and had a crazy mother. Nick wasn't gay, and Demi wouldn't be interested for long—nobody ever had been, not in Tab—and Maxi would go off to be an actress or whatever she'd decided this week, and this *was* Tab's life. Whether he got Nick or Demi was paltry. It didn't matter in the long run.

Then Nick smiled over the top of that pint glass, imperfect and stunning and unreachable, and Tab was sitting in a pub with *Nick* and not dying of fright and Nick wasn't killing him, and…

The impossibility of it hurt, and Tab wished he'd never drawn Nick, and never texted Demi back.

Chapter 17

I DON'T KNOW what to do.

It was true. Every bit of it was true, and Tab lay flat on his back on his bed, staring at the ceiling and wishing—not for the first time—that the choice could be made for him. That one of his gods would come out of the woodwork and choose for him, or upset things enough that the choice was taken away. Make Nick move to Australia. Turn Demi into a prick. *Something.*

The crush on Nick was getting too big to handle, too *serious,* especially since they'd actually started *talking* and *getting a drink together* and it wasn't just Tab staring over the desk anymore. And he couldn't possibly go out with Demi whilst crushing on Nick so badly because how was that *fair?* It wasn't. It just wasn't, Demi—anyone—deserved their boyfriend to actually like them and just them, right? So he couldn't go out with Demi.

But he couldn't go out with Nick either. Nick was straight. Whatever Demi said, and however comfortable Nick appeared to be with Tab being gay, *he* wasn't. Nick had a girlfriend, that Luce girl. There was no way forward with Nick, which meant he wasn't an option either.

And lately…lately, Demi's butterflies were competing with

Nick's. The storm when Demi flirted—when they'd…almost sexted, even though it hadn't really counted—was just like the storm when Nick came out of the changing rooms in his boxing shorts and gloves and nothing else. They were equivalent. Matched. In direct rivalry. Like…*Butterfly Hunger Games*. Or something.

About what? Sorry, at work n its a bit busy :-/

About u and the gym guy, Tab replied honestly. *I really like u but its not fair on u when I have such a huge crush on him :(and I cant go for him cos its not fair on him that I like u plus hes str8. dunno what I'm gonna do!*

And this was just part and parcel of what he liked about Demi: he *could* say that. Demi wouldn't mind him being honest. Demi was sweet and kind and really understanding, and Tab wished Nick wasn't so hot or was aggressive or a prick or…or *something,* just *something* that would kill the way Tab felt like glue every time Nick was around, and then he could go for Demi and not feel guilty or like he was missing out or…

Stop overthinking it, Demi advised.

How? Tab returned.

Fact is, u have never actually asked this guy out or if hes gay or anything. U shudnt presume. He might be. Sounded like hes flirted a bit! So he might be.

And if he is? Tab asked—because what if Nick was, by some miracle, at least open to the idea? What then? That would make this decision *worse,* because if Nick was actually remotely open to the idea, then…then…

Then who did Tab choose? If he could *really* choose, then…?

Then tbh tabby, u shud go 4 him.

Tab blinked. *Why?* he asked eventually.

Bcos lets be honest, if I could win this, I would have by now. Tab blinked. *U fancy this boxer of urs massively, ive not changed that. Kinda suggests u shud go 4 him.*

Tab simply stared at his phone for a long, long minute. Was Demi right? Nick had been there first, and his crush hadn't diminished at all since then, but…but to give up on Demi…

Would it be fair on *Nick?* If by some miracle he *was* gay, or bi, or something, then would it be fair on *him,* to date when Tab liked someone else, too? It didn't sound fair, but then…then the only option was to go for neither, and that option sucked most of all because Tab got nobody.

Don't worry so much, came a little more sage advice. *U never no wats around the corner. Trust me tabby-cat itll be fine!!!*

Im not so sure :(

ON FRIDAY MORNING Tab felt…oddly at a loose end without the portrait to do. It was in Yvonne's office now, framed and ready to go up at the exhibition. Tab wouldn't see it again until then.

Demi was being all sweet and encouraging, telling him to just ask Nick flat-out and get it over with and *he's not gonna belt u one, tabby, u'll be fine, promise!* It was nice, Tab supposed, but it still hurt. He didn't want to pick one over the other.

Maybe he could have both, he thought wildly as he doodled a morose peanut comic. It really was suicidal this time, trying to jump off that suspension bridge in Bristol. Because the peanut knew—just as much as Tab did—that there was no way he was going to win.

"Hey."

Tab jumped, dropping his pencil, and flushed as he looked up into Nick's face calmly regarding him from the other side of the desk, waiting for something. "Um, hey…?"

"I wanna pay in advance for next week's lesson," Nick said, brandishing a shabby fiver. He wasn't wearing any gloves, even though he'd already zipped up his jacket ready to leave. Maybe it had finally gotten too warm even for him. "Coming from work next Tuesday so I won't have time to find a cashpoint first."

"Um, okay, sure, let me just…" Tab dived under the table for the class list, banged his head coming up again, and then smacked his forehead off the side of the chair. Nick winced as he handed over the list, and Tab flushed angrily again. That shrine to the Goddess of Looking Cool had totally let him down. Maybe this polytheism thing had gone out for good reason: it didn't fucking work.

"You ever going to admit it?" Nick asked, printing '£3.50' in block digits before scribbling a signature next to his name.

"Admit what?" Tab fumbled.

"That you have a crush on me."

The till snapped shut on Tab's index finger, and he didn't feel a thing. He went absolutely white, the colour running out of his face and hiding somewhere around his ankles. There was a roaring in his ears like the latest NASA shuttle going up for some serious Moon time. He wanted to faint, or be sick, or just plain *die*, because a) it would *actually* be less embarrassing than this, and b) *now* Nick was going to beat him up. For defs. He even still had his gloves slung over his shoulder, ready for the putting on and the beating and the *killing Tab stone dead behind this desk*.

Maybe if he screamed really, really loudly, Uncle Eddie would get there before Nick could murder him, and he'd only have to spend a few months in hospital eating through a straw and wishing there were some male nurses…

"Is that a no?" Nick asked.

Tab sat down heavily.

"Look," Nick held up his bare hands. Oh good. He was going to do this quickly and just strangle Tab instead. That was nice of him. Considerate. It would be faster, and it would probably hurt less, because Tab had watched Nick fight, and he was *brutal*, like how he'd just tanked Allen out within a minute, and…"I…"

"I'm so sorry," Tab blurted out.

Nick lowered his hands. "Are you?"

Tab went purple. "You don't…I'm so sorry, I know it must be weird for you, and I swear I'll never do anything or tell anyone or expect anything or…"

"Right," Nick said slowly. "Er. I'm not offended."

"I know it's—what?"

"Er," Nick said again, and rolled his eyes. "Look. In my defence, I worked it out like…a couple of weeks ago. Right before the interclub. And I meant to tell you then but you started avoiding, and then when I saw you at the hospital, but you were upset and it wasn't the time, and it's really not something you ought to say by text…"

"Tell me what?" Tab said. He felt sick and confused and shaky. Something wasn't right. Nick wasn't meant to ramble and not be offended. He was meant to go nuts. And tell him *what?*

Nick took a deep breath, and exhaled loudly. "Okay," he said. "When we met, I didn't catch your name. Never did, actually. Then the other week when you were finishing off your assignment, you told me about...about Demi."

"Okay..." Tab said slowly.

Nick made a frustrated sound. "You told me about Demi. And you told Demi about this guy at the gym you like."

There was this...feeling. Like water in his legs. A sort of bubbling in his stomach, and an inching...fear. Panic, maybe. Because...

"How...how would you know...you can't know..."

Nick stuck his hands in his pockets and smiled, from one side to the other, showing his broken front teeth. Slow, small, and...shy? Maybe? "I didn't know how to tell you. I'm not...I'm not as confident as you make me out to be."

"You—" Tab spluttered, then shook his head. "That's impossible."

"Yeah, okay, tabby-cat."

Tab's brain hiccupped. The NASA space shuttle had exploded and was crashing back to Earth. His colour had given up on his ankles and was hacking its way out of the bottom of his feet to hide in his high-tops. He was going to bleed to death out of his feet.

"Tabby-cat," he echoed weakly. "Where did you...?"

Nick shrugged, still smiling. "I made it up."

"You..." Tab shook his head. "No. No, no. No way."

"Way," Nick said, and grimaced. "I only worked it out when you told me about 'Demi.' I didn't think for a minute this mate of Maxi's meant *this* gym. Or me, there's like a billion gyms and a billion guys called Nick and anyway you kept banging on about how hot this guy was. I didn't think it could be you—or me. M'not bright like that. Then when I did...yeah, well. Like I said. You were upset at the hospital and it felt a bit weird to do it by text, right?"

Tab clutched at the arms of the chair. He felt numb. He was *reeling*. Nick was...Nick was..."Right," he echoed, very weakly.

"...Sorry?" Nick offered.

"I...you...you can't be," Tab repeated, because he couldn't. This stone-faced killing machine couldn't be the same as the dorky freak he'd been texting for weeks. Could he? He didn't even *look* like...

Except...

Except in a new light, he...maybe. With a jolt, Tab realised that he'd been looking in the wrong places. Nick shaved his head, so of course he didn't have the frizzy curls. But he had the thick dark eyebrows, and the colouring. He had the same long, angled face. His teeth were smashed, so Tab had missed the smile because he'd always been drawn to what was *different* about it, not what looked the same. His eyes were the wrong colour, but how had Tab missed the way he folded his arms on counters and desks and hunched his shoulders forward, just like...

Maxi. Just like Maxi.

"Oh my God," Tab breathed.

"Yeah," Nick said, and flicked those pale green eyes to the class list still on the plastic desk. The printed one. The one that Uncle Eddie had finally typed up only a week before. "I suggest you check your list. And I'll give you a hint: my first name isn't Nicholas."

He turned and loped towards the door, hands buried in those pockets. Tab watched, stunned, and finally stood up, mouthing the *other* name to himself and called out, "You...you can't be."

Nick paused. "Why not?" he called over his shoulder.

"You're not...you're not gay. You can't be gay." It wasn't possible. It wasn't. That they were one and the same person, that Russell had been *Nick's* ex, that *Demi* had been bullied through school...

But of course he had. People wouldn't bully Nick. But they'd bully dorky, frizzy-haired Demi. Until he changed. Until he *became* Nick. Wouldn't they?

Nick twisted to eye him, and quite suddenly *grinned*. And he looked so much...so much less...*less Nick*, Tab's brain suggested, *and more...*

"Can't I?" he asked. "Well, shit. What do I do now, then?"

Tab just gaped like a goldfish. A landed one. A dead landed one. Nick laughed, ducking his head briefly and flaming a deep red colour, and then he was gone, the door clanging shut behind him, and the clatter of his boots sounding on the stairs down to the car park.

Of their own volition, Tab's hands fumbled for the class list, the page with Nick's signature the only handwritten part of it, in the same row as the neatly printed name he'd have on his boxing license, the twelfth student on the intermediate lists for next week. The list he'd never thought to check, the list he'd never actually *read*.

"Demi," Tab breathed. "Demi, Nick. Demi, Nick. Oh my God."

12) DOMINIC D. JONES.

Chapter 18

MAXI WAS PEOPLE-watching when Tab found her in the college café, lounging in her chair in an artfully sexy way, and just like the villainess Tab knew her to be. She looked casual, relaxed, oddly sexy given that Tab wasn't into girls, and horribly carefree.

And she had no right to be, damn it!

"Your brother is Nick," he said, throwing his bag into the empty chair opposite her. The clatter made a kid at the next table jump, but Maxi merely rolled her eyes at him and offered a bemused look.

"Uh, yeah?"

"Your *brother* is called *Nick.*"

"Ye-eah, Tab, I know my brother's name. What, you thought my *sister* was called Nick?"

"As in, Nick at the *gym!* The *boxer* that I've been—that I've drawn for the exhibition!" Tab shouted.

She blinked, then reeled back. "You *what?*"

"Yes," Tab snapped, and folded his arms. "So why didn't you *tell* me! I've made an absolute idiot of myself, *God* knows what I've told him, and…"

"Wait, wait, wait," Maxi waved her hands frantically. "You've been crushing on Demi?" And then half a beat later: "Demi's been *boxing?* Oh my God, Mum told him to quit ages ago, he said he was working full-time, she's going to…"

"Never mind your family domestics, *I'm* having a domestic!" Tab shouted.

Maxi whirled up out of her chair, curls flying, and seized their bags and her coat. Tab followed her furiously out of the café and into the cold, snatching his things back the moment she slowed down enough to let him. His blood was simmering. He was embarrassed and angry and—not sure why, actually.

"Okay," Maxi said, "what the hell?"

"Nick is Demi, Nick at the gym—as in, your brother, Dominic bloody Jones!"

"Dominic *Daniel* Jones," she interrupted tartly.

"Whatever," Tab retorted, waving it aside. *"Nick* came to the gym this morning and told me that I have unknowingly been venting my crush on him *to him!"*

"Mental as that sounds," Maxi held up both hands—*just like Nick had done when explaining himself!*—and frowned behind her huge glasses, "and as much as I am so dobbing Demi in it to Mum— you've been crushing on this guy at the gym *and* Demi, and it turns out to *be* Demi?"

"Yes!"

For a brief second, a silence rolled in. Maxi was staring, wide-eyed and gobsmacked, and *how had he not seen her in Nick's face before?* It was the same eyebrows-up, mouth-down, startled expression. The same 'you're fucking weird, mate' face that Nick gave him!

Then…

"Tab!" Maxi exclaimed. "Why are you freaking out, this is *great!"*

Tab stared. "Are you shitting me." It wasn't a question.

"You don't have to choose!" she enthused, and beamed. Her face was like sunshine; his felt like a rainstorm instead. She didn't *get* it, did she?

"Maxi. I have made a fucking *idiot* of myself, and Nick didn't tell me, and you didn't tell me…"

"Me? I didn't know!"

"How could you *not?*"

"How could *you?*" she shot back. "I don't watch him every day, you know, and I didn't know he'd started boxing again, he *promised* Mum that he'd quit like, two years ago, he *swore* he had, and anyway, I tried to hook you two up! I didn't know!"

"You knew his name!"

"Oh big deal, Tab," she huffed, and folded her arms under her huge breasts. "There's a *lot* of people called Nick, I don't know if you've noticed. I didn't think it could be *our* Nick! Not for a minute! Especially as he's lovely and all but he is *not* good-looking and you kept waxing lyrical about how gorgeous this guy was—I just never imagined it could be Demi! Out of all the guys that go there that could be called Nick, *why* would I think it's Demi?"

"How could you not?!"

"I don't know, same way neither of *you* two noticed!" she exclaimed. "Firstly, don't blame me for something *you* didn't notice either, and secondly, why is this a *problem?* You're crushing on the *same* guy! Twice! Just ask him out and there you go!"

"Are you kidding me?" Tab exploded. "He's totally strung me along and laughed at me and didn't tell me and—"

"And Tab, Demi is fucking dense!" Maxi shouted back. "He's *stupid!* I love him, he's my brother, but he's dumb as a fucking post and if he's known, it won't have been for long!"

"He said a couple of *weeks!*"

"Which for Demi actually coming out of his shell and *talking* to someone is like two minutes," Maxi said, and threw up her hands. "How long have you been admiring 'Nick' anyway, like a year now? Ever since you first saw him anyway. And he only *recently* started to even say hi. Are you hearing me? Demi's *shy,* Tab! He let that dickhead boyfriend get away with murder because he's too fucking *shy* to speak up! Tammy has him wound around her little finger, and God knows it's a good thing Alice can't order him about! I'm surprised he told you at all!"

"Not. Helping," Tab said, and the mental image of Nick being shy was just…jarring. It didn't want to fit.

Yet…yet the way he'd coloured when he'd confessed, the way

he always hunched his shoulders and put his hands in his pockets, the way he spoke so shortly and never for long…

It…it didn't *fit,* it couldn't be…

"Look, if he knew he should have told you earlier, I get it," Maxi said, her stance softening. "But I don't get the *deal*, Tab. The two guys you're crushing on are the same. That's *good!* And Demi likes you, he must do if he's still texting you, he talks to people normally, he's really awkward and daft, he's worse than Dad. That's why he's Alice's favourite, he always volunteers to take her places so people don't try to talk to him and Mum'll stop banging on about him being antisocial."

Tab swallowed. Hard. "He said he was bullied."

Maxi grimaced. "Yeah, well, we've established he totally fails at standing up for himself. Why do you think Mum fusses over him? Anyway! Not the point! Point is, *go for it.* You could come over after lectures today, or we could go to the bar he works at, or we could…"

"Er, no," Tab said.

"Why?" Maxi implored.

"I need to think about it," Tab mumbled.

"You're always thinking. Stop thinking and do it."

Tab didn't 'do it' so well. He knew he overthought sometimes, but…but Nick *was* Demi and Demi *was* Nick and the two didn't quite marry up in his head yet. Nick was into science fiction and bad TV shows and read stories to his disabled sister in garbled voices.

…His baby sister. Oh Jesus, the peanuts had been for *Alice.*

"I can't believe I didn't see this."

"You? I can't believe *I* didn't," Maxi huffed. "He is so busted. Mum made him quit boxing after the *last* incident…"

"What incident?"

She raised her eyebrows. They were heavy and stern. Just like Nick's. "The one where he had, like, six teeth smashed out of his face and we spent, like, a thousand pounds on dental surgery to fix up his gob?"

Tab stared. His gods stared. Across the religious realm rang a sudden silence of astonishment.

"He used to go to Hillside," Maxi clarified. "And one of the guys worked out he was bent as a burlesque dancer's make-up artist, and he got the shit kicked out of him. Mum made him quit. He told her he was just working extra shifts or there was extra training at the Army barracks!"

"Er," Tab said, his anger momentarily forgotten in the wake of that...well, *that*. "Maybe you...shouldn't tell her?"

"Fuck that, I'm going to rip him to pieces, he's been crushing on you *twice* and never told me!" she whined, and the hot feeling of betrayal began to ease in Tab's chest. Maybe Nick was—okay, Nick was *definitely*—in more shit than Tab was right now. He'd shot himself in the foot by confessing, and given who his sister was, he probably knew that.

Tab softened. A bit.

"Go for it," Maxi said, then paused. "I mean...feel free to string him out a bit 'cause he's a lying weasel and he'll be all dead anyway when Mum finds out, but...you know. Go for it."

Tab chewed on the edge of his lip, and shrugged.

OVER DINNER THAT night, Tab finally asked. Information was needed from an impartial source, which by definition meant not Maxi, and the only one who knew Nick was...

"Uncle Eddie, is Nick shy?"

Eddie looked up from his stew. "Nick...?"

Aunt JuliKate huffed. "Honestly, Eddie, the boy Andy likes."

Tab flushed. "Jones," he added. "In your classes."

"Oh, your Nick," Eddie said, and grunted. "Yeah he is."

Tab blinked. Really? Eddie knew that? Uncle Eddie was hardly *observant*. Or, you know, emotionally aware. "...Really?"

Eddie swallowed his mouthful with a wrenching noise. "Kid's a damn good fighter and gets a lot of respect in the group for it, but he's about as socially skilled as your grandmother. Wouldn't know what to say to a person if you give him a goddamn script. I had to bully him into taking his intermediate grading, he wasn't happy with mandatory sparring. God forbid he might be expected to *talk* to the other lads."

Tab toyed with his phone on the table.

"Why?" Eddie asked.

"He's…you know I've been talking to Maxi's brother?"

"Uh-huh."

"…I just found out that's Nick."

Eddie raised his eyebrows.

"He didn't know either," Tab mumbled. "But I…you know. I liked both of them."

"Tragic," Eddie drawled, and smirked. "Seems to me like you finally got a bit of luck, kid, and he ain't got the knockers his sister does. Does he like you?"

"I…think so," Tab said diplomatically, still not quite daring to believe that. Nick *was* gay. He had taunted Allen with the other guys not believing him even though Allen was *right,* and…

Maybe Nick should be in an adequate-heroes comic. The wool-puller, who could pull the entire bloody *sheep* over people's eyes.

"Then go for it," Eddie advised.

"He didn't tell me when he worked it out," Tab mumbled, toying with the remnants of his food.

"Like I said, kid struggles to know what to say after 'hello.' Go easy on him. Not everyone's bright like you. And anyway…" Eddie shrugged. "I won't say more on it, but let's say he came here because he had trouble elsewhere, yeah? Once burned and all that."

Tab flushed, still turning the phone over and over in his fingers. Trouble was right, if Maxi had told the truth. And to get Demi *and* Nick…it was suddenly, weirdly possible, and yet the unease wouldn't settle. The choice was literally in his hand. He could tell Nick to piss off, or…

Or, one of his gods murmured in his ear, *you could have the exact thing you wanted from the beginning. Two for the price of one.*

Tab snorted. This wasn't an offer in the *supermarket,* Jesus.

"For once, I agree with Eddie," Aunt JuliKate said calmly. "He's a nice boy, even if he is a complete lout—but I supposed you're used to louts with this lump for a relative."

"Hey!" Eddie protested.

"Don't take too much time over your decision," JuliKate advised. "You can't argue you felt strung-along if you do the same to him in return."

Tab flushed hotly. "He should have told me sooner!"

"Of course he should," JuliKate said dismissively. "But what do you expect, dear? He's a boy who spends most of his time being beaten up for fun. Any brain cells he had are long gone."

"You calling me thick, too?" Eddie asked with a wounded expression.

"Utterly idiotic," JuliKate said tartly, then softened. "But *my* idiot, I suppose."

Tab made a loud gagging noise and retreated from the table with his phone. He hadn't texted Demi since—oh Jesus, which name was he even supposed to *use?*—Nick had coughed up the truth, and had only received one. A simple *sorry ur mad :(* yesterday, and…nothing.

He'd been avoiding the gym, too. And it was…

He knew he was being stupid. Even his gods were telling him that, and they were usually silent and disapproving. But…

He closed his bedroom door, flicking through old text messages from Demi. He hadn't deleted them. Any of them, in fact, and wasn't that pathetic? He'd kept every last one, hoarded them like he'd hoarded Nick's voice, and…

The realisation hit him like a train to the chest.

He'd imagined Nick saying Demi's words. And he could *actually have that.*

"Fuck," he whispered.

Fuck, echoed the God of Rampant Lust obediently. Only that one turned it into a verbal order, not an expletive.

Slowly, he thumbed out one last text.

We need 2 talk. Exhibition?

Chapter 19

THE PORTRAIT EXHIBITION was being held in the town hall. The conference room had been turned into an exhibition space (through the liberal use of those fuzzy walls used in offices the world over to build employee cubicles and flexi-space) and a buffet table in the foyer outside laden with wine glasses, cheap plonk, and cheaper sandwich triangles.

Tab wanted to get drunk. *Very* drunk.

He'd arrived early so one of Mum's carers could come and take some pictures of the exhibition to show her. He liked Judith—she was a lovely, bubbly nurse who let Mum ramble and paint with her hands on everything and even encouraged the random artistic streaks—and she'd arrived, taken lots of pictures, and given him a hug.

"She'll be dead proud of you," she said, and squeezed his arm. "I mean it, love. She's dead proud of you, is Serenity. She's always talking about you, one thing she keeps hold of even when she's having one of her spells. She's gutted she couldn't come. She wants you to bring the portrait next time. You will, won't you? You going to come and see her next weekend?"

Tab swallowed against the lump in his throat. He could never tell if Judith was exaggerating, and he didn't care. "Yeah," he said eventually. "Maybe."

Judith had left after that, to take the pictures to Mum before the hospital put the psychiatric patients to bed for the night, and Tab had knocked back two glasses of wine before the examiners and the rest of the guests showed up. He hadn't invited anyone, aside from that single text to Nick. Which hadn't been answered. He'd have Maxi to talk to for some of it—not that that was going to go well—and once his portrait had been marked, he was going to go home. Uncle Eddie and Aunt JuliKate didn't do art.

He had to admit, the portrait was good—but it wasn't quite good enough. Framed and hung, he had carefully angled the viewing lights to show it off to its best advantage, and yet…it wasn't quite done. It wasn't quite *Nick*.

The raw *power* was there, in the blurred edges of the glove. The vitality was there, in the violent colours that pointillism allowed for. The technical ability was there, in the gloss-paint-flake eyes and thick wax outline. The draw was there, the focus on the subject, in the hazy watercolour background that permitted nothing else to be seen.

But it wasn't Nick. The boxer wasn't quite Nick, despite the shaved head and the intense stare. The crooked little smile wasn't there. The deadly way he stilled before he struck wasn't there. The huffing laugh and the deep, rasping voice weren't there. And it felt like it wasn't Nick because…because it wasn't Demi. Like Tab had left something vital out, and so the picture was just a picture, and not a proper likeness.

Tab hated portraits—because they had to look halfway realistic, and yet captured so *little* about the subject. His portrait showed a young man, a boxer, someone with physical strength and a powerful body…but it wasn't *Nick*.

In the end, he had opted for the simplest title possible. *Someone*. It was someone, but it wasn't Nick. Or Demi, or anybody else that Tab knew. Too much was missing for the portrait to be of somebody Tab knew.

"Tab!"

He didn't turn around.

"Tab!"

He still didn't turn around, and then Maxi was level with him, looking sultry and anxious in a long black dress and her hair twisted up in an attempt at controlling the curls. Out of the corner of his eye, he saw her hesitate and study his face before looking up at the portrait. Of her brother. Of her *brother*.

"It's really good, Tab," she said lowly.

He shrugged.

"Tab," she said, hesitated, and sighed heavily. "I *didn't* know, Tab. It just didn't click. It *should* have done, but it *didn't.*"

He shrugged. "It's okay."

"Demi said you're mad at him."

"I'm not really."

"But you're not talking to him."

"Not now, Maxi," he said, and heard a gurgling laugh from the other side of the exhibition. Alice Jones, he guessed. The guests were filing in. "You need to go back to your own portrait."

She lingered for a minute longer, but Tab refused to look at her, studying the picture intently. He could—kind of—see her point, but he was still too bruised to admit it. That *Maxi* hadn't twigged…she knew what Tab hadn't, She *knew* Demi—Nick— went by both names, even if Nick *was* a common one.

Eventually, she slipped away, and Tab exhaled. He ought to be angrier, he knew. He ought to be angry at *Nick*, but…but somehow he wasn't. Well, he *was*, he was angry Nick hadn't told him sooner, but…

But when he thought about it, Nick hadn't *done* anything to him. He hadn't been laughing at him. And he hadn't known *long*, he said so, so…

What would Tab have done, in his shoes?

"Mr. Atkinson-Barnes," a woman trilled. "Shall we start with you?"

Tab fixed a smile on his face, and turned. The examiners—a short, pudgy woman with a scoopful of grey hair clipped into wobbly place on the top of her head, and a lanky man with a wispy, thinning goatee—were waiting with the dreaded clipboards.

Tab thought about sending up one last prayer, but decided against it. His gods weren't real, and weren't going to help him. They hadn't helped before.

Let's go, he told himself instead, and nodded.

"What can you tell me?" she asked.

Tab licked his lips and opened his mouth. "It's called *Someone,*" he said, and stopped.

Because…that was all.

"It's called *Someone,*" he repeated. "And—um—that's all. He's whoever you want him to be. He's whatever you expect because, um, that's all anybody is. You see—you see what you want to see. Everyone makes assumptions all the time and we presume that someone's, um, straight or—or male, or aggressive, or even…even the person they claim to be. But we're always wrong, to some degree."

The man was scribbling furiously; the woman smiled, nodded, and began to examine the portrait. They began to whisper to each other; Tab glanced up at the focused face, and wondered who Dominic D. Jones was underneath *everything,* beyond 'Nick' and 'Demi' and 'Maxi's brother' and 'that lad' and *everything,* even his own name.

"Hey."

Tab stiffened, and half-turned, involuntarily. The examiner looked over the top of her glasses and smiled genially at the new arrival. In a heartbeat, she recognised him: "Ah," she said. "You must be the subject."

"Yes, ma'am," Nick rasped, and the sight of him was…jarring. It was jarring to see him in jacket and jeans against the backdrop of his own image, permanently coiled in raw power. Strange to see Nick *as* Demi. Tab still found fault with the drawing; he found nothing in the live subject. "Nick Jones."

She shook his hand and smiled. "Your partner is very talented, Nick," she said, before signing the bottom of her paper. "Thank you, Tennyson."

Tab flushed. Nick's eyebrows flew up. *"Tennyson?"* he echoed.

Tab blew upwards into his hair. "Yeah," he said, and grimaced. "Tennyson Atkinson-Barnes. You know. T-A-B."

"Nice," Nick said.

"Least I don't have two nicknames."

Nick half-grinned, his crooked teeth briefly showing. "To be fair, if it wasn't for Maxi, I wouldn't. Nobody else has called me Demi since I was about eight."

"You're here with her?"

"Technically," Nick shrugged. "And you asked anyway, so I escaped. Got a couple of things to say to you."

"Like?" Tab folded his arms. It was hard being angry with Nick, because…because he was a crappy liar. Tab knew that. Nick wore his mind on his face, and thinking back, Tab suspected he knew when Nick had realised, that session in the bagroom when he'd told Nick about Demi and Nick had gone all quiet for a minute. And Nick had said he hadn't known long, and Tab believed him, even if he didn't quite want to, and…

He felt embarrassed at being kept in the dark, but…maybe Nick did, too? And anyway, this meant…this meant he didn't have to choose. There was no choice between Demi and Nick because…because he'd get *Dominic,* if he decided to 'go for it' as Nick—and Demi, and everyone else—had advised.

But he folded his arms anyway as the examiners walked away and they were left alone, with only the gods listening in, because he was *not* going to cave *just like that* for a hot guy.

"Firstly, that I'm sorry for stringing you along," Nick shrugged. He looked sheepish and twice as stunning for it, and it hurt to watch him and not…not…not *react,* somehow. "Told you I'm thick. I never found out your name, see, and Luce said she'd ask for me 'cause it would have been stupid to ask after so long, only she never told me."

Tab swallowed. Luce. The blonde.

"I thought she was your girlfriend."

Nick smirked. "Well, I'm gay and she's a les, so it wouldn't last very long."

Tab bit on the inside of his cheek to not smile. He wasn't going to smile or cave or forgive, not quite yet.

"Wasn't until you said you had this crush on some guy called Demi I twigged. And it threw me. There's a lot of boxing gyms, I never thought for a second it was Grangefields. I thought it was probably Hillside, you know, other side of the college near the station."

Tab chewed on his lip. "Okay," he said finally. "But I told you—Demi—about a boxer."

"You never said his name either and anyway," Nick grimaced, "you banged on about how fit he was. I have a broken nose and busted teeth and a face like I've been in a car crash."

"You're an idiot," Tab told him flatly.

Nick shrugged again. He looked *vulnerable*, with his hunched shoulders and hands in pockets, and Tab suddenly found the two people—in his head—clicking together into one. He could see that funny, geeky kid behind the shield suddenly, and he softened.

"Anyway," Nick shrugged. "I liked you for ages, but you reacted like I was gonna hit you for ages, too, and I figured you weren't going to be interested in someone like me, not really. And anyway I didn't know what to say. I'm shit at knowing what to say, even worse since I stopped looking like a dweeb and people started crossing the street to avoid me. I figured I'd be better off going after this Tab kid from Maxi's college. He liked me. Didn't mind me being weird. And didn't know I look like this, far as I knew."

Tab bit his lip and stifled a laugh. How *familiar* did that sound? Had they literally been in the *same* situation and not realised it until now? "I..." he began eventually, and sighed. "I mean, I'm not...I'm not mad."

"You should be. A little bit."

And Uncle Eddie was right. Maxi was right. Nick was fucking *shy*, and it was weirdly...cute.

Tab shook the thought off. Eurgh. Cute.

"If I'd known what to say I would have said it," Nick said, then grimaced. "Story of my life, actually."

Tab's heart softened completely. Nick was shy. He'd been beaten out of a gym for being gay. He was brash and aggressive and confident, but it was all show, and underneath he liked bad science fiction and being a dork and pulling faces for his baby sister. He liked text-flirting.

He liked *Tab*.

Tab sighed, and the anger flowed out with the air. "How much trouble are you in?"

"We-ell," Nick shrugged. "Mum went ballistic and tried to ban me from boxing, I threatened to move out, Dad went mental because I said that, *Maxi* went nuts because God knows I'm not allowed to do anything without her knowing about it—"

Yeah, Tab could guess. Being her friend was exhausting enough.

"—and all the ruckus kicked Alice off into a tantrum, so I got in trouble for *that*, too, and then you weren't talking to me," Nick finished, and shrugged again. "So. Yeah. Loads."

Tab's mouth twitched. "Well," he said. "You shouldn't have kept it from Maxi."

"You'd think I'd have learned," Nick agreed wryly.

"Mm," Tab said, and relaxed his shoulders. "So…the other thing? You said there were a couple of things."

"Well, if you're not mad at me, fancy going out with me sometime?"

Everything paused for a moment. For a brief second, Nick looked just like his image, but in full colour: waxy streaks of beauty, spilling strength over the lines, the rubbed charcoal in the shadow of his hair and stubble, the shine and fall of his black jacket.

Then time restarted, and Tab remembered how to breathe. For the first time in, like, seventeen years, Cupid actually *favoured* him instead of leaving him to lesser, malevolent gods. And the shock of it flooded his entire system with a cool wash of confidence.

He curled his fingers into the leather of Nick's jacket, ignorant of when he'd stepped forward, feeling the coiled power in his shoulders—and kissed him.

Nick's shoulders and stubble were hard and unyielding, but his mouth was soft, smoother than Tab had imagined. Every little movement was heightened tenfold; at the seams, Tab could taste the sharp tang of citrus, maybe lemon, and curled his fingers into the leather until it creaked. He could feel a scar in the corner of the bottom lip, could feel the curve at the left that made that mouth so crooked, could smell and taste and feel and…

There was nothing, for a while, but them.

When he finally eased his fists and let go, Nick simply grinned. His hands were still in his pockets. "S'at a yes?" he rasped. And despite the flippancy and the stillness, he was flushed. And smiling.

Tab huffed a laugh, and ducked his head.

"Maybe," he said, and pushed Nick away. Nick stumbled a little, still grinning that wide, crooked, broken, beautiful smile. "Get back to your sister before she realises you're missing."

"Text me," Nick said, still grinning and walking slowly backwards for four or five paces before suddenly blowing a kiss, turning on his heel, and melting back into the crowd.

Tab sagged against his exhibit board, beaming like an idiot. His mouth tingled. His fingers were cool from the leather, and twitched with the urge to reach out and kidnap Nick from his familial obligations. Eros wasn't just *favouring*, he was actively *blessing*.

Tab fished out his phone and sent a short text. As it sent, he stared up at the mixed portrait, and found the flaws instantly. It was good, he supposed, but it didn't taste of citrus, and it didn't smell like leather, and it didn't have Nick's smile.

To: Demi J.
Time: 18.33
Message: Okay. Date/time/place?

About the Author

MATTHEW J. METZGER is an asexual, transgender author from the wet and windy British Isles. Matthew is a writer of both adult and young adult LGBT fiction, with a love of larger-than-life characters, injecting humour into serious issues, and the uglier, grittier edges of British romance. Matthew currently lives in Bristol, and—when not writing—can usually be found sleeping, working out at the gym, and being owned by his cat.

Find more online at matthewjmetzger.com.

CPSIA information can be obtained
at www.ICGtesting.com
Printed in the USA
BVHW04s0220241018
531087BV00024B/574/P

9 781515 308256